Callyhill
Echoes of Change

*Dear, Patricia
with every good wish,
love + hugs
Mary B xxx xxx*

Mary T. Bradford

978-1-915502-96-4

All rights reserved. ©2025 Mary T. Bradford

All intellectual property rights including copyright, design right and publishing rights rest with the author. No part of this book may be reproduced or transmitted in any way including any written, electronic, recording, or photocopying without written permission of the author. This book is a work of fiction.

Published in Ireland by Orla Kelly Publishing.

Orla Kelly Publishing
27 Kilbrody,
Mount Oval,
Rochestown,
Cork,
Ireland.

Praise for Callyhill, Echoes of Change

"With this collection, Mary Bradford, a tremendously empathetic writer, has crafted a beautiful and essential piece of work. Stories weave into one another to conjure a striking vision, panoramic in its scope and yet finely distilled, that at times harrows desperately close to the bone of today's Ireland. The characters who populate these pages are the down-at-heel and put-upon, living small but for all that thoroughly worthwhile lives, and it is the searing reality of their portrayals that give this work such an exquisite and precious humanity. A book we should all read."

Billy O'Callaghan, (Life Sentences)

"They're wonderful stories, composed with elegance and compassion, of people seeking refuge, safety, and that elusive thing, home. A beautiful and heartening warmth radiates from them and Mary's writing, as always, shines with an awareness of the complexities of the heart, the fragility of life, and the strength of the human spirit. Sad, funny, beautiful, ultimately hopeful."

Donal Ryan, (Man Booker Prize Nominee and winner of numerous other awards)

'Poignant, tender, loving and devastatingly truthful, Mary Bradford's stories capture the essence of Ireland today.'

Patricia O'Reilly (The First Rose of Tralee)

Contents

Go, Be Happy 1

Mr. Perkins 11

The Birthday Party 23

Dear, Mom and Dad 35

Aleksy's Wedding Day 46

Special Delivery 57

Hey, Paddy 68

Enough is Enough 80

The Crochet Circle 92

A New Homeland 105

A Tough Workday 113

Michal 124

For The Reader 138

About This Collection 139

Please Review 140

About the Author 141

Other Books by the Author 142

Acknowledgements 145

Go, Be Happy

When it's dark, monsters and demons creep about and cause mischief. My father, Baba, told us about them during story time. Then he would tuck us in at night so no baddie could grab our toes. We were safe. But now it is just me and Baba.

My sister and Mama died the day the bomb fell. The news said it fell in the wrong part of the city. We were sitting at the table for dinner, Mama with her back to the window, my baby sister in the chipped high-chair next to her. A pot of bean stew that Mama makes best was on the table, and I watched the steam curl and squiggle into the air. The highchair had been mine. But I am nine now.

When the window wall behind them exploded, they did too. The broken glass, the crushed walls, remind us every day of the danger we live in. The outside looking in at us, watching how we go about in our wounded house. I don't like the war. I asked my friend one day, what the war was for. But she could not tell me and said, "Amira, the bold men fight, but they don't care who they hurt."

After the bomb broke our house, Baba said, "We are leaving to go live in a happy place. It's a long way away, and it's not easy to get there."

I want to be happy, so I nodded and told Baba I want to go there, too. People came to our crushed home and Baba sold them some of our furniture – anything they wanted, they could have. One of Baba's friends drove us to the coast. Outside the car, he shook hands with Baba, and then he patted my head and said, "Go, be happy."

***

My ears still hurt. Bombs can make your ears sore. Sometimes I cannot hear everything people say; other times, I don't want to hear what is said. I don't like the cold. I am squeezed in between Baba's legs, my arm is wrapped around one leg and I hold on. My head rests on his tummy. There is no room here. Everyone is shoved up on top of each other, and I feel sick.

I peep over his knees and see faces that look frightened, like me. They are older, and still, they are anxious, so I think I am not such a scaredy cat after all. Baba's arms rest on my shoulders, his thumb twisting my hair. Mama always loved my curls. She said it was because I ate all my dinners that I had shiny, curly hair. My sister had thin hair, wispy little threads like torn cotton.

"It is okay, Fatima," Mama would tell her. "When you eat all your dinner, you will have long, thick hair like Amira." Then Mama would smile at my younger sister and hold her little fat cheeks in her palms and whisper how much she loved her. Fatima would chuckle when Mama did this to her.

Fatima was a happy little girl. Baba said I was the best big sister to help Mama mind the baby, but I didn't mind helping. I loved Fatima. Mama had been a bit sad before she arrived, now Mama was almost always happy. Only the war stopped her from being very happy.

The boat lurches, and the frightened faces around us are staring at everyone around them. This orange boat is cramped, and tonight the sea is in a bad temper. I hold Baba's leg tighter. He has pulled his knees up towards him.

"Hush, Amira, hush little one. It will be over soon. You are a brave little girl." His words are sweet honey to me. I listen to them and store them up inside of me. When I cannot sleep, I think of them, and they are my lullaby. We are a team now. We look after each other. Mama and Fatima are a team, too. They watch over us.

The water surges up, up, and crashes down. Its salty taste forces itself into my mouth, adding to my sickness. Some of the people not holding onto the ropes are swished around the boat, and they fall on us. I check to see if Baba is holding on and he is. An arm is stretched out behind him, like he did when he sat on the sofa watching the television. His fingers grip the thick, dirty rope; he even has it wound around his wrist. He sees me looking at his hand and he smiles down at me.

"We are going nowhere, my daughter. I am holding on for the both of us." Another big wave hurls itself at the boat, and as I turn my face into Baba's tummy, it engulfs us in seconds.

It is so cold.

We are tossed left and right. Right and left. Up, then plunged down. Down, then thrown up. I try to think happy thoughts, but they are jumbled in my head like the sea is inside me, flinging the thoughts around while it plays with our boat.

The screaming has stopped, along with the calling out to the prophets, and some to a God I do not know. I must have fallen asleep, because now it is day, and the sea has become tired. It is still and quiet.

"Where is my boy, my boy? Have you seen him? He was here beside me." A frantic cry from a woman wakes others as she searches among the crowded boat. She is one of only a few women sailing with us.

"Sit down, you will rock this raft and more will be lost." I think he is the sea captain, but he doesn't have a hat.

Her boy is not on the boat. I cannot hear any cry looking for his Mama, but I hear her wailing and screeching. No-one tells her to stop. We all have lost loved ones – if not on this small boat, then back where we lived. It is better she gets her sorrow out and throws it to the wind than carry it inside her forever. Being sad eats you up from the inside out; it wraps around your lungs, then you cannot breathe. It squeezes your heart and then you cannot love or live again.

That is what the holy man said when we buried Mama and Fatima.

Soon, when the woman has stopped her crying, the man beside my father said, "Thank goodness, her voice was scratchy like a seagull, only more annoying."

Baba grinned; his teeth are yellow, and they make him look ugly.

The morning is still breaking over the horizon. I watch the sun rise in a quiet gentle way, its orange and purple glow warming the sky to the east, stretching itself into a new day. Clouds in the distance start to shuffle across this skyscape. They are white and fluffy, and I lay my happy thoughts on them hoping Fatima will see them and be happy, too.

With his free hand, Baba hugs me to him. I close my eyes and go back to sleep before the next storm riles up to attack us.

***

"Amira, watch your little sister while I finish the dinner." Mama *is in a happy mood. Her mother is visiting today, and she will be staying with us. I love Nan Iman. I tickle Fatima, catching her toes and pulling them. She laughs and sticks out her feet for me to do it again. Her laugh is making me laugh, and I roll on the floor. She laughs more at me then. So, I make weird faces, sticking my tongue out and pulling my eyelids down, but this scares her, and she stops laughing.*

"Amira, Amira, what is so funny?" My Baba's words wake me from my dream, and I sit up, looking to find my baby sister. I want to tell Baba I was playing with Fatima, but then I remember.

The sun is above us now. It has moved from the east and, like us, it is going west.

"How long more must we drift like this?" an old man with a red scarf shouts out to no-one but the sea. Others mumble and mutter their answers. Yet no-one knows the right answer.

"All the money we paid, for what? To be let die. I was foolish to believe false promises. We all were. Tell me, how much did you pay? I bet you feel stupid, too." Others near him nod.

"Shut it. There is no need to speak like that. You will frighten the children. We are not doomed. It has been three days, not 30." It is the sea captain again. His voice tries to be happy, and he smiles while he is speaking.

"The children need to learn the truth. This world is filled with bad people. This boat is filled with lives that were better back in our towns. Now it is filled with death waiting to claim us." The man wipes his face with his red scarf.

Baba lifts my face to look at his. He whispers to me, "That man has given up, little one. Do not listen. His eyes are already dead; it will not be long before he will be, too. But we are not like him. It is important we believe. Do you believe, Amira?"

"Yes, Father. I believe. We are going to be happy again, like the holy man said. To see the beauty from the hill, you must first climb it. The stones and the fences to step over along the way is our sea now." My smile is one of certainty and love. Love for my brave father.

"Amira, you are a very wise girl. You will grow and thrive in our new homeland. You will see the beauty in this world, because you will have climbed many hills and mountains, and you will conquer them. Remember that." Baba's eyes mist over. His face, full of kind wrinkles, looks down at me.

The sun spreads its heat across the water, claiming it and turning it into a desert. In a desert there is no water; in the sea there is only salt water, so it is no better. I pull my green scarf over my head. My face is hot, my clothes are itchy, and they are marked with white lines. Baba explained it is the salt from when the storm drowned us with wave after wave. Now the heat has taken away the water and left these tiny lines. I start to count them.

While cuddled into Baba, a tune Mama sang to us comes into my head, and I begin to hum. Baba joins in on my song, and then another man joins us. In a little while, others have started to sing, too, and we are all happy, like we are at a party. Even the woman who lost her boy is drying her tears and listening.

The day is long. Baba fiddles in our backpack for food. He finds some biscuits and breaks one in half, and we share it. The crumbs are dry on my tongue. It is hard to swallow dry biscuits without a drink. Then Baba shares two biscuits with the woman near us in return for a swallow of her bottled water for me. I take a small sip and offer it to Baba, but he shakes his head and tells me to drink up.

"Baba, tell me about our new homeland." I push my legs out before me and turn to face the other way. Moving is hard. Most people are leaning against someone else.

"It will be a place of peace. You will go to a school with lots of new friends. I will work in a new office like I did before, and at the weekends we will go to the parks."

"And have picnics?"

"Yes, and picnics. You will not be sad again, only on the day we remember your mama and Fatima."

I reach up and rub my fingers over his chin, slow and definite. Then I laugh, "You will shave every day, too, Baba."

Some of those nearby laugh with us. On the boat, everyone hears what is said. There are no secrets.

In the evening, silence has become our blanket. Many are sleeping. The warmth of the day is leaving, and a small breeze blows over us. The boat is bobbing along, each wave a soft ripple; it is not so rough now. Baba yawns and squirms around until he settles against the edge of the boat. Then I hear his soft snores. I pull his jacket closed across his chest and hold his hand. Our bag with some food is tucked in beneath him. It is safe.

Lying against Baba, I look up to watch for the first star. I play a game with myself to guess where in the evening sky it will appear. The clouds have moved away to make room for the night, and a black shawl is being pulled across by the sun as it settles down to sleep. Soon there are many stars. Bright and shiny, they fill the darkness like sparkly freckles. I wonder if Mama and Fatima are awake, or are they sleepy and snug in their bed, too.

"Night, Mama. Night, Fatima." I blow a kiss up to them. I see it travelling in the air, a shimmering streak of love going up and up until it is lost in the stars.

It is the pain in my tummy that wakes me. I need to pee, but I don't want to wake my Baba. I try to hold it, but the pain gets stronger. The cold at night does not help. I glance around, everyone is sleeping. I have no choice but to let my pee escape. Its warmth is welcome as it spreads down my thighs and soaks my clothes. But I know shortly its coldness will be uncomfortable, and I will not settle again until the next day dries me once more.

***

"How many days now?" a voice from the corner asks.

"How many days what? Since we got on this coffin, or to when we hope to get off?" another shouts. But no-one answers, because no-one knows how many days it is either way.

We are all hungry now. Day and night are no different. The starry sky is not beautiful anymore; I hate how they twinkle down at me, high above me, happy and light. The sun has burnt my legs and my face. I try to cover myself with my scarf, but it is not thick enough to stop the hot rays from scorching my skin. Everyone is in a bad mood. There are grunts and groans and the sea captain keeps saying, "Any day now. Any day we shall see land." I think he has gone mad, and he never knew how to sail the boat.

Baba looks old and tired. He is getting weak. His hands are no longer able to grab the rope tight. He tries to be strong when the sea has another tantrum and wants to turn our boat upside down, but his hands now slip, and we are thrown on top of others. I hold his jacket in my fists, and I pray to Mama and Fatima. I think about the day Baba promised to take me to a new life. I was happy then. A new life away from the bombs, the shooting, the fighting. But death is all over the place. It is back in our old town, and it is here on this boat.

A man at the other side of the boat died yesterday. He didn't move when someone told him to shove away from them. I watched two men strip him and check his pockets. But they were empty. They took off his shirt, his shoes, removed his pants, and then his socks, but left his underwear on. Then they folded the clothes into a pile. It looked like a dirty, soft pillow.

Baba moved over to help them lift the man and throw him into the sea. They said some words, and then Baba crawled back to me and held me tight.

"I love you, Amira. I am sorry." His voice is broken. He smells of sadness.

When I think of my young sister, I feel annoyed. She is not here with her tummy hurting. I bet she is playing with new friends in her new homeland. I think there is lots of food and drink where she is. And she has Mama to sing to her every night. I hate that. I hate her. Why didn't I die that day? Why did I get to be here with Baba, and she doesn't?

My tears run down my face, and I scream. A big, howling scream, and the pain and the fear that has lived inside me like a snake slips out into the ocean. Baba is trying to calm me, and he can't stop me. I beat his chest, I close up my fists, and I hit him. I try to hit him hard, but my fists are small, and I do not have the strength to keep belting him. I shout out, "I hate you. I hate you."

Trembling from my sobbing, I sit next to Baba. He does not try to hold me. He knows he cannot make it right for me. I must cry and be sad. Then I will be ready to climb the mountain again to see the beauty.

That night, the wind runs around the boat. Its laughing frightens us as it grows stronger. It begins to play with us, tossing the orange raft one way then another. Now it is stirring up the sea. The water laps the edges, then it sneaks over, and we are once more facing a storm. I look at Baba and cuddle into him.

"I'm sorry, Baba, I don't hate you."

He hugs me close and whispers, "I know, I know."

The wind is angrier than the sea, and the boat almost turns over. People are screaming. Wave after wave fills the boat with water as it splashes around our feet, our bodies, and soaks us.

Baba loses his grip on me and falls away. I reach for him and miss. The wind and the sea are now very angry, and they crash into the raft together.

I see the boat being swept away from me. I splash and twist to look for Baba.

Then I see him. Leaning over the side, reaching out to me. Far away. Men are pulling him back.

I sink down.

I cannot see Baba now; he is just a shadow. I no longer splash.

The darkness has me in its clutches. It wraps around me, it pulls at my toes, and I am sinking deeper.

Mr. Perkins

She sat on a concrete bench with only a crow for company. With a glazed reflective eye, the lone bird tilted its head to study Rosa. It appeared to be listening, then straightened its neck and took two steps closer.

"Got nothing to say then?" she asked, as the cars sped by on the road. Reaching into her bag, she searched for food, a biscuit, crumbs, anything to give to her feathered friend. She found old, crushed cookies still in their small plastic packaging. Danique at the café had placed the pack next to her coffee when Rosa had called in for her daily cuppa.

"Here, you have it." She mashed the two biscuits and scattered them on the ground close to the bird. "Are you on holidays or do you live here?" Embarrassed by her behaviour, Rosa looked around to check if anyone was watching her talking to a crow, but no-one was in sight.

The bird just pecked at the crumbs. Once it had its fill, it cawed in thanks and flew off.

Rosa's wristwatch showed 10.45. Fixing her hat and picking up her bag, she left to go about her day. She'd never noticed a crow here before. There were gulls, doves, pigeons, but few crows – unlike in Ireland, where they ruled the roadways.

Rosa ambled back to her apartment. One of many habits she stuck to since moving here was to avoid the midday sun whenever possible. Being Irish, she burned to a crisp if caught in the noon rays.

Living on the Mediterranean coastline was good for her. Slipping off her sandals once home, the cream floor tiles were soothing under her feet. She would go and rest.

A new beginning, a fresh start, her family echoed over and over when she'd shared the news that she was leaving. Her moving away had been a sigh of relief for her mother, a decent night's sleep, one less worry. At the time, it didn't dawn on Rosa that it was so. But with no-one taking up her offer to come visit, she accepted her absence was pleasing to them; that it was what they wanted.

Eight years since she had seen her parents, Rosa had not returned for her mother's funeral three years ago. A brief note told her about the woman's passing, but there was no invitation home enclosed. Sleepless nights had followed. Should she or shouldn't she return? Would her brothers and sister want her to be there? She had decided no.

And now this, another message. This morning's news bothered her, an unexpected dilemma to be sorted. The letter on the table was coffee-stained, a jam thumbprint showing where Rosa had held it. Her aunt's handwriting was neat, the words calm and measured. The aunt wasn't putting any pressure on her, but she did want Rosa to know about the situation at home.

Sliding beneath the crisp cotton sheets, Rosa slipped into her siesta.

***

In the cool of the evening, she sipped a sparkling water, lemon slices floating in the glass. The Marina Café was busy, music playing at the right level so people could still chat without having to raise their voices. Tucked in a corner, she watched the life of the locals and tourists play out before her. The café hummed with family. Children ran to and fro, their tiny feet in pretty sandals, mothers and fathers checking on the little ones every so often. Laughter, the shouts from children, meals being shared surrounded her. Dusk gathered overhead, evening clouds darkening, the sun glowed red, sleepier as it dipped in the horizon. The sounds of the restaurant faded.

"Rosa, Rosa, come on, it's time to come in. Bedtime." She saw the slight woman at the front door of their house. Living on the outskirts of a village, the green fields around were their playground.

"Soon, Mam. I'll be in soon."

"Now, young lady, and I won't warn you again. School in the morning." Her mother's tone told Rosa not to argue. When Mam put her hands on her hips like she was going to draw a gun, it meant she was serious. Without hesitating any longer, Rosa ran for home.

"Want another water, Rosa, or maybe something stronger? It is, after all, the weekend." Danique winked as she cleared a table.

"Maybe a vodka and tonic, Danique. Please."

"Give me five minutes and I'll join you. I'm finished here for the night, thank goodness." The waitress continued wiping tables and pushing chairs back in.

Rosa nodded. She never tired of observing others. Not being involved suited her. Moving here had been a decision made in haste, but she didn't regret it. She had enough regrets without adding to them.

Squeezing her eyes shut, she tried to conjure up her mother again, but failed. The moment had passed. She pinched the bridge of her nose, and a pained expression flitted across her freckled face.

"Are you alright?" Danique placed two large drinks on the table, pulled out a seat, and sat opposite Rosa.

"Fine, fine." But Rosa's voice softened, losing power as she folded her hands across her chest.

"Hey, I've seen you like this before, so spill. No, don't! You've had contact from Ireland, am I right?" Danique took a gulp of her vodka, grimaced at the bitterness, and swallowed it loudly.

Rosa winced at her friend's words and found she could not meet her gaze.

"Are you working tomorrow?" she asked after a brief moment.

Danique shook her head. Rosa knew that it was not in reply to her question, but rather in sadness of her avoiding the truth. They drank in silence.

The revellers began to depart, the ripple of the water against the boardwalk becoming the back drop as the families said goodnight. Other bistros began to tidy up, stacking chairs, pushing tables closer, and finally pulling down the shutters.

Danique and Rosa strolled arm-in-arm along the marina. The summer night was warm and humid as the perfumed scent of the bougainvillea enveloped them from behind white walls on their route home. No more was made of Rosa's sadness brought by news from home, nor her reluctance to discuss it. Danique knew she would share in her own time.

The next morning, Rosa picked up the letter again and reread it. Her father was being put into a nursing home. He'd suffered a stroke, adding to his Alzheimer's. Rosa's aunt thought her niece should know before he deteriorated further and maybe wouldn't recognise her, should she visit him. A new nursing home had opened back in Callyhill. Butterfly Gardens, it was called.

'*Isn't that a lovely name?*' her aunt remarked in the letter.

Rosa longed for the years before *it* happened. Before hell opened its doors and swallowed her family. *Untouchable* – that horrid word – the word her mam had used. Feeling the pull of tears, she straightened her back and drew a deep breath in. No. It was not happening. She had dealt with all that, and now she was in a happy place. Alone but happy.

"What hour do you call this to be coming home? With the Foley fella again, were you?" Her mam sat at the kitchen table, her dressing gown pulled tightly over her night-dress.

"You should be in bed, Mam." Rosa's whisper did nothing to placate the older woman.

"How can I sleep when I know the town is talking about us, about you and your carry-on?" Her mother spat the words while her fingers fidgeted with her rosary beads.

"Go to bed, Mam."

"Always an answer. Look at the face on you, you bitch."

Rosa winced at the sharp words and left her mother to her prayers.

The cawing outside called to her and she stepped onto the balcony. Across the road, sitting on a satellite dish, was a crow. "Hey, Mr. Perkins, are you stalking me?"

Where had that come from? she wondered. *Mr Perkins?* She laughed at her own silliness, but she thought the name suited the bird. Going back inside, she picked up some *pan de payés* and a small bowl of water. She placed the water on the circular table on the balcony, then tore the crusty bread into pieces and laid it next to the drink.

"There you go, Mr. Perkins. Breakfast." She returned to her living room and waited. Would he fly over?

The bird watched her from across the street, its head twitching from side to side, those cold eyes studying the scene. She was just about to give up on him when over he flew. First, he landed on the railing, balancing, his tail feathers going up and down to help him steady his stance. Then, with his chest puffed out and a gangster's swagger, he strutted along the ground, moving unhurriedly yet deliberately towards the table. As Rosa watched him, she remembered her father telling her that crows were very intelligent. They remembered faces.

"Imagine that, Rosa, they know who feeds them and who harms them. And listen to this now, it's genetic, it passes on to the next generation. So, if you see an injured or dead crow, stay away, because the others will think you're the one who harmed it. Isn't nature great, my pet?"

Her father's large, hard-working hands were generous and kind, always helping family and others. She pictured him now – in a wheelchair, her aunt had said – old and unable to do even the smallest thing for himself. Thinking about his walks through the fields, checking the cows, fixing the gaps in the ditch, his couple of whiskeys in the evening by the fireside, the timber he chopped burning bright, now all gone for him. These days not only was he confined to the nursing home, but his mind held no memories. The pensive feeling dissolved as she needed to get on with her day.

Mr. Perkins was perched on the railing.

"Okay, I'm off. See you later." The bird twitched its head to the side.

Her shift at the *supermercado* started at two, so she would pop in to Danique at the café first for lunch.

The women's friendship had blossomed from the moment they met at the apartment gateway. Rosa had been struggling with suitcases when the dark-haired woman offered to help. The woman's arms were covered with butterfly tattoos, and long feathered ear-rings adorned her ears. She seemed so exotic to Rosa.

After settling the young Irish girl into her new home, Danique had invited her for a cup of tea. They had chatted and bonded over many more shared pots of tea over the years and become firm friends.

"You do know the whole place is gossiping about you? About us? If your father won't talk to you, I will. I'm not going to let you shame this family. A married man! I'm telling you know, you're not to be meeting him, and don't think for one minute he loves you. He's using you, and you a big fool for him."

"He does love me, Mam. He's leaving her soon, and we're going away. Together. Now you know, and you can't stop me."

"Stop you? Stop you? I'll be glad to see the back of you and the disgrace you are, an untouchable. Ha, he's leaving his wife! He is in his arse leaving his nice cosy home, a good wife who has his shirts crisp and a hot dinner for him every day. Leave that for a child who can't boil an egg. I said it, a child! That's what you are at 17 years of age. Even Father Jones can't make sense of it."

Rosa recalled recoiling at her mother's merciless words; even now their hurt still pierced through her core. A coldness shot through her, and she shivered.

Danique brought over a small tomato and olive salad to where Rosa sat. "How are you feeling?" But she felt she didn't need to hear the answer. Her friend was pale beneath her tan, and circles lay beneath her eyes, casting shadows.

"Dad's had a stroke, so he's being put in a nursing home on account of having Alzheimer's too."

"Oh, that's sad to hear. But a nursing home might be for the best, don't you think?"

Rosa didn't reply, she didn't know if it was for the best or not. Trying to picture him sitting all day unmoving, built inside her. A nausea sat in the pit of her stomach, and she trembled at these thoughts of his incapacity. He had been her lighthouse through it all, never wavering in his love for her. When it had all gone wrong, he'd placed his arm around her and told her she would always be his daughter. Then the train had pulled into Callyhill station, and he'd placed her bags on it for her. *How had she forgotten this?* she wondered. *His love, always there wrapping itself around her. Protecting her.*

"They're heavy," he commented. "Get help lifting them off," he added. Not meeting her eyes, he drew her to his chest and kissed the top of her head. "Mind yourself, my Rosa. Your aunt is waiting for you. It's only till the baby is born. I'm sorry, pet."

She stood watching him walk away, shaking his head and muttering under his breath.

***

"Are you going to see him?" Danique asked gently.

"Is there a point? If he doesn't know me, why bother? Anyway, I didn't travel for Mam's funeral, and they didn't miss me then, so why would I go now?" The hot drink scalded Rosa's throat and she coughed and placed the cup down.

"He loves you. You often said it."

"But the others, Danique, what would they say? I don't want a scene. Not one of my siblings kept in touch. Why should I go back to be treated like a leper?" Bitter tears welled up, but she brushed them swiftly aside. She would not waste time or emotion thinking about them.

"Forget them. Don't even tell them you're coming." Danique turned to serve a family who had called out to her.

Rosa sat looking out at the sea, a deep moody blue, the sun sparkling on the surface cutting it like a broken mirror. *Could she do that? Slip in beneath the radar. Just a quick two or three days?* Her mind drifted as the water lapped the beach.

Rosa reclined against the kitchen door. Her heart fluttered and ached at what she heard. "It's for the best," her mother's words stung.

The priest sat at the kitchen table, a large slab of buttered teacake before him. His cheeks full of it, crumbs fell from his mouth as he tried to talk and eat. "She'll be well looked after. Other girls who've fallen from grace take this path; a charitable place where she'll be with her own kind. Then, once the baby's born, it can be dealt with, and Rosa can get on with life. These homes give the girls time to reflect on their... behaviour, change their thoughts to those more pleasing to God."

She stroked her stomach. Empty now years. A little girl, Deborah. Ten minutes she'd got to hold her; ten minutes before she'd been swept away from her like you'd brush some dirt out the yard door.

"Hey, Rosa, if I knew any better, I'd say that bird was staring at you," Danique laughed.

"Mr. Perkins, you followed me."

"Ah, you're talking to birds now, is it?"

"Mr. Perkins arrived a few days ago."

"You do know they are an omen."

The two women looked at the crow. The crow looked at the two women.

"Maybe it's a sign, Rosa." Danique shrugged her shoulders.

"A sign of what?"

"They're a messenger of sorts." Danique stepped away to continue serving others.

Rosa stood to leave, filled with thoughts of her friend's words about Mr. Perkins having a message for her.

***

In her apartment, nestled in the sofa in her pyjamas, Rosa sipped a coffee. With work over and now watching the evening sun set, she grappled with her thoughts. The cawing alerted her to Mr. Perkins' presence. Opening the balcony doors, she stepped outside to find the bird sitting on the railing, his gaze piercing into her soul. *Dad*, she thought. *Could she visit?* Fear gripped her, stopping her from trusting her decisions. Her heart thumped at every thought of the journey back.

Usually a quiet man, her dad hardly spoke, yet when her mother had brought Father Jones up to the house to advise them, her dad had not held back. She heard her father's words once more in the kitchen at home.

"It is not my daughter who has fallen from grace. What about the married man who made her pregnant? Where's he in this? Breaking all his vows and more. No! No daughter of mine will be put in a home when we, her family, can take care of her."

"Listen to yourself, nonsense and rubbish. She'll not stay in this house. Either she goes to the home or goes to England. Sorry now, Father, but there's more than one way to deal with a bastard," her mother's voice shook the room, seeping venom and hatred under the door and out the windows.

The sound of her angry father's fist on the wooden table rippled through the house. "I'll take her to my sister's. She'll be cared for there with kindness and compassion. Your heart will blacken for those words. Your memory is short, woman." He stared at his wife. "Were you not with child when you took my name?" Rosa gasped at his words and ran up to her room.

**

The flight home filled Rosa with anxiety from her toes to her head. She couldn't relax, and refused the offerings of the stewardess to eat or drink. Her heart pulsed in her ears while she tried to still her thoughts. She carried a small bag with enough in it for three days, and a return ticket.

Butterfly Gardens was bright and homely, she was comforted to see. His room was painted in a pale green, like leaves unfurling in springtime, and there was a nightstand with some photos near the bed – photos of her siblings' weddings, and one of her as a child. The empty wheelchair was parked close by.

Her father lay napping, the blankets tucked up around him. His skin was grey, eyes shrunken. He looked so small lying there. She took his left hand, thin and weak in hers, and clasped her fingers tightly around his.

"Dad, I'm here. I came to say hello. You stay sleeping… I'll wait." Her words were less than a whisper in the already silent room.

She sat thinking, dreaming, wondering how it would have been if she had kept her baby. "Granddad"; the word settled on her lips. He would have loved her child, his granddaughter. Rosa bent down to his ear and whispered, "I named her Deborah," then sat up watching him breathe.

Outside the window, she heard a familiar sound. She recognised the call. Mr. Perkins had brought her home.

Her father's fingers moved against hers and a slow smile spread across his lips. "Rosa, my Rosa." He stirred and released a deep sigh, then settled to sleep once more.

The Birthday Party

Ned leant back against the low stone wall, his hands crossed over his chest. This wall had seemed so high when he was young. In those days, he would stick his toes into the nooks and his fingers would grab some piece sticking out, then he'd pull himself up to see the fields that lay on the other side – a world not yet explored at seven years old. He would watch his dad working, checking on the cattle, mending ditches after a storm. Other times, his dad – pipe smouldering nonstop – would walk the land in solitude.

Today was Ned's sixtieth birthday. His two brothers were here with their families, as were his own daughter and his two grandchildren. Joan, his wife, had wanted to throw a party in the local hall, but Ned had rejected the offer. To keep her happy, he'd suggested a family tea party here in the orchard, like they had when he was young, and his mam would bake cakes and prepare fancy sandwiches. Joan, happy to be marking the occasion, had made a list of what needed to be done.

The day Joan agreed to marry him was when he became the richest man in the world, he believed – and he still thought so.

The heat of the sun was kept at bay by large branches, the sunlight dappling in between the apple trees, shadows stretching across the trimmed lawn. Bees flew around the blossoms, and the smallest of the grandchildren and nephews and nieces ran in and out through the trees. His mother had loved her orchard. The kindness in her smile had softened the wrinkles, while lines etched her tanned skin from always being outdoors. At the side of the orchard was a small vegetable patch she used to tend –

now Joan's responsibility. She and Joan had lived harmoniously side by side since he'd brought home the young bride almost 40 years ago.

How had he gotten to 60 so fast? Where were the days he had kept putting off to go and explore life outside Callyhill? He'd had plans, and so had Joan. Plans to visit cities, relatives. And now look at them: celebrating a milestone birthday with their family, without fulfilling those dreams. He hadn't set foot away from this farm to see what his child and brothers got to see and live. He'd never had that freedom. It had been snatched from him. Innocent youthful days grabbed along with his ambitions, thrown on the manure heap behind the abandoned barn where all things no longer needed were put.

"Ned, come here. We need you to cut the cake," Joan called out to him.

Without fuss or bother, she had organised the full day, baking, batch cooking, and cleaning the house so it would look perfect for the family returning. This was the home place for Ned and his two brothers. He was the eldest; they were two and three years younger than him. Joan always fussed when they decided to visit, maybe once a year, because she wanted them to know that the home was still welcoming and in safe hands since their mother had died six years ago.

Ned, though, told her not to worry what they thought, as they had both scarpered off once they'd turned 18. If they wanted to relive their youth, he told her, they could look at old photographs.

She would scold Ned for this, but he didn't understand why it was important to her: they had left. This home was hers and his, and they could do what they wanted and change whatever they fancied, whether it was knocking down walls to make the kitchen bigger, like Joan dreamt of, or even selling the place and the farm. It was theirs. As far as he was concerned, his brothers could shove any notions that they had a say about it up their arses and feck off to London and Florence, where they lived.

He rambled down to where the tables were set up and sat in the first empty chair he saw. The grandchildren were excited to help Grandad blow out his candles, and he loved their exuberance. Their young companions wanted to get in on the act, too, so to keep it fair, Joan had baked two cakes. One for Ned and their small ones, the other for his brothers' grandchildren.

"One, two, three, blow… Happy birthday to you, happy birthday to you, happy birthday, dear Dad, Grandad, happy birthday to you." The chorus of cheers lifted into the air, and the scream of the young children added fun to the moment. Balloons swayed in the party atmosphere.

"What did you wish for, Granddad?" Eddie asked, squirming onto his lap.

"No, Eddie, he can't tell us. No, Grandad, don't tell us!" The panicked voice was Eddie's older sister, Sarah. She lived a life of unicorns and castles, and Ned smiled at her worried little face.

"Of course I can't tell. Eddie, some things can't be shared, and birthday wishes are one of them." He looked at his granddaughter, her eight-year-old face visibly relaxed. Her brother, five, cuddled in closer to his chest, not caring any more about wishes, only about being on Grandad's lap. "There will be no milking the cows with me today, Eddie, but the next day okay?" Ned whispered to the young lad.

"But… but… but I love my cows."

"I know, pet, but this evening you will be tired after the party. The cows will still be here waiting for you."

How Ned loved the grandchildren. Their futures were bright. Their mother, Ned's daughter, was videoing the gathering. But now that the important cutting the cake was over, the camera was put away and it was time to enjoy the day. Joan had made the rule: no phones once the cake was cut. She said people wanted to relax; not fear a camera stuck in their face, recording every moment. And Ned had agreed with her. Memories were best when they were shared in storytelling, in moments of conversations when someone would say, "Can you remember?" or "Who was it?" Everyone had their own memories, and today would be one of those times.

The afternoon played out with games and laughter. The old swing, with its ropes almost part of the strong branch it was tied to, was the cause of small arguments if the occupant stayed on too long while others waited their turn. Ned's own daughter was sitting on a picnic blanket with his nieces and nephews, catching up on each other's lives. It was a happy gathering, and Ned took in all around him, the family scene of scattered generations together.

As the early evening approached, the young children were gathered up by their parents and bundled into the cars. It was time for going home; it would be their bedtime soon. Jim and Mike, Ned's brothers and their wives, stayed on. Just the six of them.

"I'm off to milk the cows. Be back once it's done." Ned stretched and wiped his hands along his thighs.

"Did you not get someone in for today? Take a break, Ned. Sit down." Jim's English twang stretched across the table to where Ned now stood.

"I had a great lad, a Polish man called Michal, but it didn't work out." Ned's glare was hidden by his strong, bushy brows. If Jim bothered to look up, he would have realised that he irritated Ned.

He looked at Jim, a belly groaning out over his belted trousers, a large measure of whiskey in his glass. Then he looked at Mike, the youngest of them. He was chatting to his wife, pushing his glasses up on his nose. Ned decided to continue with his task and turned from the table.

"Really, Ned, this is a milestone. We often thought we'd not see this age when we were younger, considering Dad bowed out at late, what, thirties?" Jim spoke louder this time.

"More tea anyone?" Joan asked. She knew her husband's moods by his stance, and right now, his shoulders were stiff, his hands fisted by his sides, his back to the company at the table. "I'll wait 'til you return, Ned, to make you an Irish coffee. You deserve a few for your birthday. Okay, love?" Her voice was calm to his bubbling annoyance. Soothed by her words, he walked away to the milking parlour.

Ned changed into his overalls and wellingtons. The cows were lined up waiting to be brought in. He knew each one like he knew each blade of grass on the land.

"Hey, girl." This Friesian was always first. Leading the way for the others, she flicked her tail and mooed gently, waiting to go to her stall for milking. Ned loved the animals – each one with their own traits; the leaders and the followers. Once the machine was running, he went about doing other jobs.

This was his life from early dawn to dusk and throughout the night at calving time. The job engulfed his every moment, and it had been that way since he'd stepped into his father's role at 12 years of age.

Jim's words niggled beneath his skin, the slight English accent a touch too far for Ned this evening. Sitting on a stack of pallets, the memories of his father's sudden death was always with him, his uncle's hand on his shoulder as they stood by the coffin. "You're the man of the house now, Ned. Be a good lad and help your mam. It's up to the two of you to keep the farm."

And he had. School had been over, his friends lost. Running the farm had taken over every part of living. Ned didn't go to pubs; he could not afford a hangover. "The cows don't milk themselves," his mother's words rang in his ears. But an unexpected night off had led to him meeting Joan at a table quiz.

Once his tasks for the evening were finished, Ned joined the others and sat listening to the conversation while Joan made him an Irish coffee. Smiling and kissing the top of his head when she placed the hot beverage before him, she whispered, "Relax now and enjoy the few hours left."

The state of the world was being discussed, with Jim and Mike comparing their cities, nodding at each other's words, and sipping their whiskey. Their wives chirped in now and then about the hassle of airports and the cost of college for children.

"Don't mind the children, I had to go back to college just to keep up with the young whipper-snappers in the office. Got my Master's last year in Business." Jim slapped his leg, and a murmur of congratulations ran around the table.

"Did I hear Callyhill has a new councillor?" Mike asked.

"We do. It's Sheila, one of the Nugents from Flood Street. She's not afraid to tackle any issues either. Gets herself into hot water now and then," Ned replied.

"What issues could be that bad for a small town? It's not like she's the Mayor of London, is it?" Jim laughed.

"She stood up against a proposed direct provision centre late last year. Divided the town, so it did." Ned watched Jim and Mike look at each other.

"Typical small-town thinking. Keep the foreigners out," Mike mumbled.

"Do you think?" Ned asked. Although he agreed that the narrow-mindedness of a small few could dictate if they shouted loud enough, he did not reveal this to the men.

"Glad I got away from here," Mike continued, and Jim nodded at his brother's words.

They sipped their drinks, the whiskey bottle emptying bit by bit.

"Well, I'm delighted to hear that. It makes my life easier knowing it." Ned broke the sunset silence.

His brothers sat upright in their seats and waited for him to explain. Joan said she felt a chill and asked the other wives if they'd like to go inside for a glass of wine. The trio left their husbands to it.

A woodpigeon called in the distance. Fairy lights that Joan had hung around the orchard patio twinkled as the day became sleepy. The balloons freed by the children were now tangled in some branches.

"I'm selling this place," Ned announced quietly.

"You mean the land? The farm?" Mike asked. His eyes never left his oldest brother.

"The lot." Ned, startled by his own words, looked at the men and tried to gauge their reaction to his declaration. They looked like they were about to cry.

"As in, the house, too?" Jim put his whiskey glass down.

They waited for him to speak; even Ned wondered about his decision. But nothing came. Laughter from within the kitchen reached the men's ears and broke the bewilderment that fogged up their minds.

"Callyhill is home. It's our anchor. Are you sure you want to sell it?" Mike's face was melting with sadness.

"You both know you've got a site each below, near Murphy's bridge, in the east field. Why can't you build a holiday house and still visit the place?"

"This is home, Ned. You can't just take that away from us. This is where we grew up, our childhood, memories, this… this place made us." Jim was now sitting forward, leaning on the table, this revelation of the night creeping up him like a black shadow.

His older brother watched, guessing Jim would stand up to make his point, but the whiskeys had him doubtful if he could.

Ned threw back his chair and stepped away. He daren't say anything in case of regret in the morning. He had learnt how to take the measure of a situation and then act accordingly. He was letting his own words sink in. They were filling him up; he felt a... a... freedom.

He turned to his brothers who were still looking like lost toddlers. Right now, he hated them. *When would he stop being the father, their father? Who did he have to look out for him?* He walked away towards the low stone wall, the apple scent lingering, softening the thoughts inside him. The picnic blankets from the day lay beneath the shelter of his mother's apple trees.

"I think you're being selfish, Ned. I think you should've asked us our thoughts on it." Mike had followed him.

"Is that so? Why?"

"It's our home, too. Well, not quite on paper, but in here." The youngest of them pointed to his chest.

"He's right." Jim had joined them.

Ned walked on and found his spot by the wall. It was the place where he would spend the end of most days looking back at the house, his home. A cow lowed in the darkness, Ned's scent reaching it, telling the animal he was nearby.

Now, tonight, Jim and Mike flanked him. All three facing their youth, the house they had shared for many years.

"Listen to me now." Ned took a deep breath. "I know you have your memories. I have mine. Tell me, Mike, what do you remember of Dad? I bet nothing. And you, Jim, what's your recollection? Very little, I'd imagine. Well, I'll tell you mine. I remember a man who died before his time. I remember being told I was the one now to help our mother. I was 12, lads, fucking 12, and I was told to be a man. I couldn't cry for my father like ye did. I had to be strong, to step up and take over. I did it, too. I was up and out while you two snored in your beds each morning, and I was last to bed at night."

"It's not our fault Dad died or that you're the eldest," Jim snapped.

"Did I say it was? I'm telling you that I sacrificed to keep this place going, to help Mam."

"Sacrificed? Ned, you got to own the place, you got it all." Jim took a few steps with his arms outstretched, then twirled.

"I never asked for it," Ned growled.

"Well, you didn't say no either," Mike said.

"I don't remember any of you asking for it? The few bits you did around here at the weekend were boring chores for you, interfering with your studies, your friendships, what you were asked to do for three or four hours on a Saturday. I've done all day every day as my life. Who asked me if I wanted to be a farmer? Who asked me if I wanted to be taken out of school at 12? Don't you think I had dreams? Don't tell me here and now that you had hard lives."

The cows could be heard rustling in the field beyond, spooked by the raised voices. Their breaths in puffs and snorts reached the orchard. The stillness of the early evening was gone. Crows overhead called out as they retreated to their nests for the night.

"Oh Jesus, the poor me story, is it? If you had balls, you could have left when you were older. No-one would have stopped you. You never said anything about being stuck here; you never said it to me, at least." Jim slammed his hand down on the wall, its print marking the green moss on the stones.

"Christ, Jim, you did nothing but say how you were going to go to college and leave this shithole, isn't that what you call our small town? Don't you see, you and Mike got choices? Neither of you even thought about Mam. How would she keep the place going without one of us being here?"

"Ned, if we took it for granted when we were young, it's because you made it so. You can't blame us for having lives you wished for. It was you who got stuck here, fair enough, but that's only because you were the eldest. It could have been any of us, if we were the first born. If you sell this place, what will you do? Where are you going to live? Whether you like it or not, this shithole, this town, Callyhill is your blood. What you want was what you never got. The grass is always greener. Living in Florence is beautiful, I know. Sounds magical, but I work bloody hard for it. I may not be from dawn to dusk stuck in cowshit, but I work hard too for what I have. So don't go making out we took your youth from you. I refuse to be blamed for something I had no part in." Mike strode towards the house.

"Walk away all you like. But you were the one that didn't want me to sell the place earlier. You are the ones romanticising the place. If you love the place so fucking much, buy it. You're not being cheated out of your memories. Like you say, your life is in Italy, so fuck off back to it and leave me to live mine." Ned's words spat into the air, a breeze lifting them through the leaves up to the night sky.

Jim followed his young brother. The birthday was over.

Ned stood alone, watching them leave. Flashes from the mornings they walked down the passageway to the school bus collecting them, the day they walked down the passage for college, for London, for Florence, the weeping of his mother as she watched them go.

Tears stung him, rolling over his cheeks as the car lights disappeared from view. He cried for lost time, for his taken youth. *They didn't understand*, he thought. They didn't get the loneliness that shadowed him each day in the fields, his cows the only ones to hear his spoken thoughts, fears, longings. Maybe Mike was right; maybe he hadn't had the courage to walk down the passageway, too.

He would talk with Joan, hear her words on the matter. He wouldn't sell, of course; little Eddie was coming up behind him. But it was time for him and Joan to live a different life.

A rustling behind him made him turn, and he spotted his cows lying on the grass contented. He no longer needed to climb the wall to see over.

Ned stood. Once more, the sense of freedom washed over him. He was looking out again, looking at his choices, his dreams once more opening before him.

He would no longer look back.

Dear, Mom and Dad

Katie slipped her key into the lock. She was tired after her night shift. Hearing the cries of the Jacksons' baby next door, she prayed it wouldn't keep crying. A nice cup of tea, her fluffy pyjamas, a hot water bottle, and her duvet were all she could focus on now.

Sandwiched between the Jacksons and the Dabrowskis, her one-bedroomed flat was clean yet boring. She didn't have spare cash to brighten it up, so she combed the charity shops for cheerful prints. So far, her favourite find was one of sunflowers. The yellow faces made her smile no matter the Irish weather or how hard the shift at work had been.

In the small, dim living room, Katie had hung two photographs. One of her parents; the other of her sister Janelle and her six-year-old daughter, Ami. Two years she had been in Ireland now. Katie was lucky; she had a job, a place to live, and was able to send money home. Money for her niece, Ami.

At two-thirty the shrill scream of her alarm woke her, but she had slept well. Her bed was cosy, and the Jacksons' baby had obliged her by not crying. She lay for a bit longer with thoughts on home. Her sister's death was still raw to linger on, but Janelle had never listened, and now little Ami was motherless. First, Janelle had tried to hide the bruising, but then she'd no longer cared who saw the marks on her.

Their elderly parents battled as hard as Katie to help their older daughter. But when Janelle's boyfriend pushed their father to the ground and threatened to have the house burnt down, the bully had won. They were too old to take him on. Not long after that, Ami had cried all night and prevented him from sleeping. He shook the little one and screamed at her to shut the fuck up, while Janelle, terrified for her daughter's life, begged him to stop. So, he did.

Then he started on her, and he quenched her life.

The radio from the Dabrowskis' flat broke through Katie's thoughts. She was happy with the intrusion; her tears would have fallen once more, as they did every time she thought of her sister.

Her stomach rumbling got her out of bed, and she heated up some soup and made a toasted sandwich. She was due on duty at eight in the evening, so she showered and wrapped up against the October cold then went out.

The street was busy with people bundled up in scarves and gloves, woolly hats pulled down tight on their heads, coats buttoned up. Katie liked this frosty weather; it was cleansing. Pushing open the door of her favourite café, she glanced about for an empty table. Spotting one, she stripped off her coat and scarf and laid them on the chair by her chosen spot.

The girl behind the counter waved and told her to sit, she would bring over her usual order to her. Katie did as she was told. A few minutes later, a large coffee, with two biscuits on the side, was placed before her. It was nice of the girl to remember her; it made her feel like she belonged. Callyhill was not quite a city, but a large town with notions, her workmates often commented.

Katie sat back and watched the toing and froing of the many customers. It was a pleasant place. The tablecloths, with their tiny polka dot pattern, matched the curtains at the large window to the front of the premises. Back home, cafés weren't that much different. The buzz in the warm air was uplifting, scones, croissants, sausage rolls, and pancakes, their warm aroma lingered, and the hissing of the coffee machines with the spurting of the burco boiler gave the impression of a beehive – busy and nonstop.

Loud teenage girls came in, the open door allowing the cold air to race through the café. Their over-tanned bodies looked more orange squash than sun-kissed brown as their laughter and rough chatting cut the comforting feeling of earlier.

Katie turned away from them, casting her eyes towards the window. She knew how easy it was to be accused of sticking her nose in by only looking at some people. Some saw her as different; not one of their own.

She pulled out a book she had in her bag – an autobiography of Gerald Durrell, the zookeeper. She loved reading, and one of the residents where she worked, Aleksy, had encouraged her to take his books once he was finished enjoying them. She was grateful for this kindness, as it meant her money could be spent on more pressing needs.

Butterfly Gardens was a nursing home with over one hundred residents, and the staff worked shifts in three 12-hour slots. This evening, Katie would work from eight until eight the next morning. There were other workers from the Philippines, like herself, mixed with Indonesians and a few Irish.

Katie's schooling back home had been cut short after Janelle's death. As she needed to earn to help raise her niece, it was thought best that she should go abroad to work and send money home. Then, when it became too much for her elderly parents to keep Ami, the young girl would come to live with her.

The teenagers in the café were growing noisier, throwing straws across to other tables, tearing up the sugar sachets, and spilling the contents on the table tops and floor. Some customers told them to behave, but the young ones just shouted back at them. The waitress who had served Katie walked over to their table and asked them to leave.

"We're only having fun. What's your problem?"

"You're loud and littering the shop. You've not ordered anything."

"So?"

The waitress stood there. "You're taking up seats that paying customers need."

People held their breath waiting for the youths' reply.

"Fucking dead-end place anyway, only for ould wans fit for their graves. Ould piss bags." A bleached-blonde girl pushed her chair back and stood up. "C'mon, girls, this place stinks."

Katie looked over her shoulder at the scene.

Too late.

"What you looking at?" The blonde rushed over to where she sat. She pushed her on the shoulder and placed her face before Katie's. "I asked you a question."

Katie remained silent while the waitress came and stood beside her. Two other waitresses were now out in front of the counter.

"Coming here and fucking taking jobs from us. Shove off back to the hell hole you crawled out from, d'you hear me?"

"Get out." The waitress spoke in a firm tone. "I'm calling the Gardaí."

"Yeah, typical, stick up for this bitch but throw your own out."

As Katie moved on her chair, she didn't see the teen grab the milk jug. Within seconds, the contents had been poured over her head. Without looking back, the gang of girls ran from the café laughing and yelling, giving the bleached teen leader high-fives in celebration.

Silence replaced the warm feeling of earlier, its stillness cold and uncomfortable. Customers and workers remained motionless while Katie picked up her things and left to return home.

"I'm sorry, so sorry," the waitress shouted after her as the door closed.

***

Her parents were old. They couldn't grasp using mobile phones, and when Katie sent one to Ami for Christmas, she hoped the young child would quickly learn how to use it. Unfortunately, it had been snatched from the child's hands the moment she showed it in public.

Her parents preferred letters anyway, they said. But Katie would have loved a face-to-face video call. To look into her mom's brown eyes, see the smile full of wisdom, and know she was well, was all the young woman sought, and her father, healthy and coping, would be blissful to look upon. But no; a letter it was.

Dear Mom and Dad,

Ireland is cold right now, very cold. But the warmth of most people makes up for it. There are a few who cause trouble, but those people are everywhere, right? Work is good. I love the name Butterfly Gardens even though I've never seen a butterfly nearby. Some of the residents remind me of Nan and Pops. I like it there. Wouldn't it be wonderful if you and Dad could come live here at my workplace? I would take care of you each day. I would brush your hair and wash your feet. I would make you your food, and all you would need to do each morning was get up. And each night, sleep with the sweetest of dreams. Ami would be happy in school here, I know it. I know I'm dreaming, but I'm allowed to dream, aren't I?

I'm making friends but I don't go out much. It is better to save for our future. Anyway, going out is expensive. I'm reading a lot, which you know I enjoy. Soon it will be Christmas. I shall post Ami's gift next time. I've enclosed some money for you. I know you say not to, that what I send through the Post Office is enough, but it is just a little extra for yourself. Buy some nice siopao, and take a break with some hot chocolate to wash it down.

I'm missing your cooking, Mom, and your storytelling, Dad, but that is a small thing for when Ami grows up a clever girl. I shall write again soon. Send me some news, too. Love you, and hugs to little Ami.

Katie xxx

Her fingers clutched the thin paper as she stuck the stamp on the envelope. Part of her heart travelled home with each letter she wrote. The man behind the post office counter always smiled and asked after her parents, how they were doing, and wondered if she would get a chance to return home for a holiday. He had a kind word for everyone he served at his hatch.

Katie's shift started in an hour, so she strolled towards the care home. Swathed against the frosty evening air, she kept her head down. Today's drama with the milk had been rare, but not uncommon. In queues, she would sometimes be jumped over or a dirty look thrown her way. It was easy to push her, as she was slight. Other times, on the buses someone would spread their body over two seats, and if she asked them to move so she could sit down, they would smirk and ignore her. Rarely would anyone else come to her aid. It was best to stay out of these incidents, to mind your own business.

Although homesick, even now after all this time, she knew the feeling would pass. It came in waves, usually when she was tired or had had a difficult shift at work. Her workmates were kind, inviting her to the many parties they threw – especially karaoke nights – but she was shy. And when she kept refusing, they stopped asking. Janelle had always been the pretty one, the party girl.

Katie was happy to keep under the radar and work, get Ami a good education, and be a good daughter to her parents. But there was one boy who had caught her eye at work. He was her opposite – blond, pale skin, and warm green eyes – only visiting her in her dreams.

In the locker room, as she placed her bag and jacket away for safe keeping, Katie heard the girls whispering about a resident's daughter arriving unexpectedly.

"What's going on? Is there trouble?" she asked Poppy, who had the locker next to her.

"No trouble. Just that old guy in Room 16 had a daughter turn up out of the blue. No-one knew she existed, apparently.

According to the day-manager, she was kicked out of home years ago for having a baby. Imagine being kicked out of home. Sure, if that was the case now, there would be more on the streets than living in houses," Poppy laughed and wandered off.

Some of the others whispered about this Rosa arriving and making her father so happy. A peace had swept through him since her visit, and he was more contented somehow, the staff said.

Katie thought about how understanding her parents had been when Janelle had announced her pregnancy, and the love they showed for Ami. Not everyone was so lucky, she guessed.

Changed into her work tunic and pants, Katie went about her routine. She liked the silence the night brought. Aleksy had been full of chat, asking if she was enjoying the book, sharing stories of war-torn Poland. She listened, often with tears slipping down her cheeks. His longing to go back to his own country was heart-breaking, even though he'd lived in Ireland for most of 60 years now.

The stories some of the residents shared reminded Katie of the Philippines, tales her grandparents told. The world was not so different after all. Sorrow and tragedy, joy and happiness, were to be found in equal measures.

Once everyone on her list had been seen to, the night passed without incident. The walk home took a little over a half hour, and she decided to stop in at the café from yesterday to grab a coffee.

"Oh, love, I'm really sorry about yesterday. I thought we'd never see you again." The assistant greeted her with a warm chocolate croissant and coffee, and said it was on the house.

Katie thanked the woman for the gesture and, having eaten, was reluctant to leave. A sense of belonging hung in the air, and the soft chat and breezy banter between staff and customers wrapped around her. Sleep called and, having relaxed in the café, her limbs craved their rest.

A little ache in the pit of her stomach rumbled as she faced the silent interior of her flat once more. Loneliness drifted in as she closed the door behind her. Some days she wanted the Jacksons' baby to cry and the Dabrowskis to blare their music until she could bear it no longer. Other days, she planned to fly back to her parents and forget about her responsibilities to them and to her niece.

If only, she thought, while hugging her duvet around her chin and her toes wrapped in their fluffy socks. If only Janelle had not died; if only she didn't have a duty to her parents, to her niece; if only she was rich and did not need to worry about spending; if only she had a boyfriend who treated her like a queen. On and on it went until her mind could think no more if only scenarios, and sleep quenched the troubled girl's thinking.

It was at the Christmas party that the blond boy who Katie liked asked her to dance. She nodded with shyness, and he led her to the dancefloor. Then he asked her for another dance, before offering to get her a drink. Afterwards, he walked her home and said goodnight with a gentle peck on her cheek.

Katie giggled when Poppy teased her at work. But secretly, the young woman was thrilled. He had brought her to the cinema in the New Year, and twice asked her to go to lunch with him. Soon, facing the small flat after work became easier, and the long evenings and the warmer weather caressed her life with hope.

Sitting by the window and looking out on the daffodils in the small patch of grass around the street lamppost, Katie began a letter home.

Dear Mom and Dad,

I pray this letter finds you both well, and Ami also. Christmas this year was not as lonely as I thought it would be. Maybe I am settling better to life here. I still long to be with you, and I hope to have saved enough to return maybe at the start of next year for a holiday. Work is the same, and I am making better efforts to meet my friends. Don't worry, I shall still send home money. How could I not?

My whole life is for young Ami. But it is nice to be living some a little here, too. Resident Aleksy, who shares his books with me, is dis-improving as the weeks go by. He believes he is in Poland now, rather than here in Ireland. It is sad to watch, but I read to him a little each shift.

I will write again soon. I might have some good news for you in the next letter – a nice surprise maybe. I want to see how things go for now before telling you too much. See how I tease you, Mom? Ha-ha. (Yes, it's a boy, a nice boy.)

Love to you all, and hugs to dear Ami,

Katie xxx

The post office was busy, a queue slithering along the gloomy room. Katie looked around her; several, like herself, were sending money home. This brought strength to her, knowing she was one of many.

Hurrying out the door once her business was dealt with, Katie spotted him waiting for her. Leaning against a shop front window, his hands dug deep in his pockets, he toed the ground beneath him. She called out to him. He strode across the street, a wide grin lighting his face.

A smile radiated her joy as he pulled her in for a hug. *Maybe Ireland could be home after all*, Katie thought.

Aleksy's Wedding Day

He slipped his feet into the red tartan slippers. They reminded him of his childhood Christmases. Next, he reached for his walker and pulled himself up from the bed, then stood still for a count of ten.

Aleksy had been told this would help ground him, and not to rush into the morning. In other words, they were afraid he would fall if he hurried around. As if he could rush at his 90 years of age; it took all of 15 minutes to get to the bathroom and brush his teeth! Aleksy shuffled over to the bedroom window and drew back the boring beige curtains.

Life had become all rules and regulations.

He looked out to the heavens, a favourite thing of his to do. The sky fascinated him with its colours and shades, its moods and shadows, whether the day would be happy or gloomy. This morning, although still dark outside, the dawn was breaking on the horizon. A pallet of orange and purple greeted him. Broad brush strokes swept across in soft lilacs and bled into the sunshine orange that promised to push and start the day ahead.

He drew in a deep breath. Something important was happening today. It was the lavender shadows that jolted him. Yes! Today, Aleksy was getting married. His Magda had managed to seek out a pale lavender handkerchief for him, to match the ribbon she would wear tying up her brunette curls. They had been excited about the fortunate finds, especially since the town was a wasteland of rubble. No food to be got, hunger at every turn, but his Magda had found some material, enough to brighten this special morning.

Love swelled in his chest, and he straightened up, ready to wed his sweetheart. He needed to get going, to wash and shave and polish his shoes. He turned and headed to the bathroom.

"Morning, Alex, good to see you're up and about." Katie, the care assistant, started to pull at the covers on his bed. She plumped up the pillow and folded back the top blanket, humming sweetly as she went about her day. He had not heard her enter his room.

"I'm getting married today!" Aleksy stopped by the bathroom door. "But keep it quiet. Magda doesn't want fuss." He raised a thin, bony finger to his lips and winked.

They had not told anyone of their plans for the wedding. It was not quite a secret, but there was extensive poverty after the war, people were struggling just to get through each day, so to be getting married was ridiculous. But he and Magda wanted to be together. The war had denied so many of so much.

"Are you now? Getting married, you say. Well, we need you looking your best for Magda then. How about I help you with your shave and pick out your best shirt?" Katie placed a gentle hand on the man and guided him to the sink.

"It's at the small church by that awful war office, if you want to pop in."

At breakfast, Aleksy sat with other residents and slowly ate the porridge with fruit that was placed before him. His wedding thoughts were now tucked in another niche in his tired brain. Norman, across from him, was finding it hard to eat without his teeth. The soft milky mixture slipped down his chin as his shaking hand directed the spoon to his mouth.

"Can you get new ones?" Aleksy asked.

"No. They won't get me any more teeth. Said I keep losing them, but they have to be here somewhere." Norman sighed.

"Ask Katie to help. You will starve otherwise."

Norman stopped trying to eat and looked at Aleksy, who was shaking his head with memory and mumbling. A sadness dripped into the air between them.

"Yes, those were the days. Did you go fight?" he asked Norman, while placing a hand on his own stomach. Not waiting for an answer, he muttered on, "It was hard in my home country. We struggled; such sad times. Many days we had nothing. Nothing but dirty water. I knew one man who would kill the rats and try to disguise them for his hungry children; he told them they were eating little pigs. The rats were huge and were certainly not hungry, they ate everything. If you were dying, they would be there before you closed your eyes."

Katie walked up to the table and grabbed a napkin to clean Norman's chin. "Alex, what are you saying? You will turn Norman off his breakfast. Why not go to the day room if you're finished eating?"

Once the men were up and mobile – Alex with his walker, Norman with his dark brown walking stick – she sent them off towards the communal day room. Residents were gathering there to listen to the news, read the papers, or have a chat. Each had their own chair. They never changed where they sat from one day to the next.

The two men sat down. Sometimes at this Senior Club, there were new people, and it took him awhile to remember their names. Aleksy looked around and wondered if he knew anyone. One woman over by the piano wanted to sing, but another woman was asking her to stay quiet.

"This should be interesting, Norman. Look at the two over there, like children in a playground." He pointed at the two women and started to chuckle. Ever since Magda died, he had been calling in here every Thursday. It got him out of the house, and he liked the company, even if a few of the old dears were a bit loo-la.

"Who's up for some bingo?" A young girl in a green tunic had come in. She pulled a table out from a corner and began to set up the ball machine. There was a pleasant murmur of agreement, and the two warring women went silent and took their seats.

Aleksy smiled to himself. How clever of the young girl to trick the women into behaving. Everyone loves bingo, and he resolved to compliment the girl when the game was over.

Sheets of different colours were shared out amongst the residents, along with pencils. Then, once everyone was settled, the bingo girl started up the machine to mix the numbered balls.

"Okay, today we are starting with the white sheet. This prize is for a line – four euros. Any line once all the numbers are marked off. And what do we shout if we do that?" She put her hand to her ear and waited for their response.

"Check!" the old people chorused.

"Right. First number out is, key of the door, 21, two one." Her voice was clear and loud.

A silence occupied the room while number after number was announced. After ten minutes, anticipation of a win seeped in. A few grunts and sighs rippled as each player waited for that vital ball-call.

"Top of the house, 100."

Shuffling in seats lent to the restlessness.

"Legs 11, one, one."

"Check!" The room exploded into exhaled breaths and some minor swearing.

Next up was a full house. This was serious; the money increased to ten euros.

"All eyes down again as we start the next game."

The morning passed in fun and dismay, as coloured sheet after sheet of numbers were marked in circles, strokes, and boxes coloured in.

"Right, tea and coffee time, and more bingo next week. Well done to all our winners." The girl busied herself with tidying up, and the residents chatted amongst themselves.

Aleksy stood up and pulled at his jumper. He straightened his clothing and looked down at his chair, then patted his trouser pockets and again looked around.

"What are you looking for?" Norman asked.

"My scarf. I had it with me when I came in. Maybe I left it with my coat, hanging up. Oh well. I'm off home. See you next week, I'm sure. Bye now."

He shuffled along, saying his goodbyes to those he passed on his way from the room. The hallway was long but bright. A sunny lemon was painted on the walls, and framed floral prints dotted the walkway. He moseyed on, admiring the gardens through the locked windows. The day was clear, frosty, and sparkling. He had definitely worn his scarf. He would never have come out on such a cold day without it.

A door opened and a care assistant stepped into the corridor.

"Excuse me, I can't find my coat and scarf. Do you know where they could be?"

"Alex is the bingo over?" she asked.

"Yes. I'm off home now, but I've mislaid my coat."

"Let's help you find it then." She smiled and, guiding the old man and his walker, they both strolled the rest of the hallway. A pleasantness lingered between them.

"What is your name?"

"Linda." The young assistant pointed to her name tag as she spoke. "I love your name, by the way. I think if I had a boy, I would call him Alex."

"Do you know why my name is Alex?"

"Tell me."

Linda and Aleksy settled themselves into two armchairs placed in an alcove. The old man was glad to sit down. At times the walker was cumbersome, and his arms got tired handling it.

"Well. When I first arrived here to Ireland, there weren't many of us around. I'm Polish, as was my dear wife, Magda. 1948 we arrived. Poor, frightened, broke, but together. It was close to Christmas, and when I tried to get a job – odd jobs, of course, nothing grand; anything so we could have money to eat, you see – the Irish kept getting my name wrong. I didn't mind. Many pronounced it as Alex, so I left it that way. I became Alex, and I also got a job. All long ago now." He shook his head with memories, his voice breaking as he pulled a hanky from his trouser pocket and blew his nose.

"You were in Poland through the war?" Linda's eyes were wide with disbelief. For her, the war had all happened in her schoolbooks, in films, on television. Here was someone who had lived it, had survived it.

"Yes. Much was taken from us. We were not allowed to think for ourselves, even the smallest of decisions. We lived from day to day, and at times, hour to hour. I don't like to talk about those times. Magda and I said we left it behind and that's where it would stay. It was easier to do that than to remember our lost family and friends. Are you married, Linda?"

She shook her head, unable to take her eyes off this man seated next to her. Alex was a favourite resident, always polite and with a kind word to all the staff. Never had she realised his difficult past. Watching him now as he remembered life before, she saw his years, his forehead lined with age, his eyes bright but without life, a sadness that peeped through even when he smiled.

"Do you and Magda have any family? Children?"

Aleksy sat back in the velvet covered chair. He stretched his legs out before him, the red tartan slippers catching his eye.

"Christmas is for children, isn't it, Linda? A happy time for families. When I was little... I had a sister, by the way. She and I were close. We were much loved, and although my parents weren't rich, she and I wanted for nothing. We were happy, Linda, and lucky. But of course, as children we didn't realise it, and some would say, nor when we grew up. One of the things we children got every Christmas were new slippers, red tartan, and a book each. Magical times. But to answer the question, my dear, no."

He appeared deep in thought, small sighs escaping as memories flashed into his eyes, and she longed to hear more.

"Am I keeping you from your day?" he asked.

Remembering his sister and Christmas stirred bruised moments. He should remember more, share more with others, but not having Magda by his side, he carried loneliness, making it hurt. He was reminded of their decision – a difficult choice, but for them the right one. He glanced at his young companion. Her eyes were shining, her youth beaming back at him. Her soft, clear skin blemish-free of age.

His wrinkled hands, dotted with ugly brown liver spots, clutched the arms of the chair. His skin paper thin, almost translucent. Where were the firm, strong hands that had pulled away bricks and stones from blown-up homes?

"Are you tired? Would you like to go to your room?" Concern filled her smile.

"Well, you asked about children. Magda and I thought about that for a long time. The morning we married, the small church was a heap of stones and rubble. It was bombed a week before our wedding day. Anyhow, we stood amongst the grey dust, broken pews, and scattered stained glass, and made our vows. We didn't know when the war would end; often it looked like it never would. But it did, and we got a chance to leave and start anew. We arrived here. But you don't live through those dark years and not have scars, deep and hurting wounds all inside you, not ones you can wrap in bandages." He beat his chest and then tapped his head, as his words wafted into the air around them.

Closing his eyes, he inhaled a long breath, holding it as he shook his head. Then in a soft, low whistle, he let it go. His breath rattling his chest, Aleksy raised his head and wiped a single tear that had slipped down his right cheek.

Linda wanted to reach over and touch him, but she hesitated. This was his time, his life. Her interfering would not change it, not ease what was still piercing his heart. She could only listen, give him her ear, allowing his words and thoughts an audience.

"We agreed not to have a family. Why bring new life into a world where evil could rise fast? It could happen anytime, and we had lost our family, our community, our whole life bombed, broken, ripped from us – in some cases, by people we knew in pre-war days. So no, no children. We wept for days after that, seeing young families in parks, shops, all around, but always we believed it was the right choice." Some colour flushed to his face. "Forgive my words, but when we made love, we had to be careful… unlike now. There are many ways to stop having babies."

Chatter from a side room broke out to the corridor where they sat. Linda stood up, and with gentleness, bent down to Alex and hugged him.

"Thank you. Thank you for all that you've shared." Her own eyes misted over, and she had a lump in her throat that she tried to swallow. People appeared less welcoming nowadays to others from abroad.

He responded with a single nod to her thanks, leaned back once more, and closed his eyes. She went and got a blanket from a nearby cupboard and placed the navy cover with tassels across his knees. She tucked him in and then stroked his head. She stood near him, letting him settle and relax, while the chatter around them wandered off.

A little snore escaped, and Linda realised Alex was asleep. She left him to it and went to find Katie. Each assistant had certain rooms under their attention and was responsible for that resident's care. She found her workmate and told her that Alex would be not at lunch as he was sleeping.

After some time, Katie came to check on her charge, but he was not seated in the armchair. She went looking for him. A sing-song had started up in the communal room and a handful of the residents swayed to the music. Those who could manage a few steps danced in a circle like children. Aleksy was not with them.

She wasn't too concerned; security was of a high standard in the home. Still, it was unlike him to share about his life during the war with others, and the thinking he was getting married this morning niggled at the back of her mind.

Katie herself knew what it was to be homesick and lonely, no matter how much time had passed since arriving in a new country. Her parents back in the Philippines depended on her for money. She continued her search.

"There you are, Alex. I was looking for you." Her words were whispered, even though he was the only one present. Standing beside him, she offered up her own thoughts in the silent prayer room. Letting him be for a few more minutes, she then spoke. "Come now, you must be hungry."

Standing proud, he kept his stare on the altar before him. He reached out to a vase of flowers that stood by the feet of a statue, and picked a flower. Then he turned and smiled at her and handed it to his new bride.

"You look beautiful, Magda. We did the right thing. Once we have each other, we have everything, my love."

Holding the flower, Katie and her companion left the oratory. Without fuss, he went and had his meal. Time ploughed by. A bit of television filled an hour or two for Aleksy, but his mind was elsewhere. The pretty sky this morning had unsettled him, and memories had flooded the day. He didn't like remembering. Yet that was all he did lately, remember. The darkness of early winter evenings cloaked the sky, and lights popped on in rooms.

Back in his bedroom, he paused before he drew the curtains closed. No stars winked in the cloudy blackness outside. Patches of dark grey battled with the last wisps of the day's light, the evening sky taking its turn to tell the world to sleep.

After the bathroom, he fumbled with his shirt buttons, folded his trousers on the chair, and readied himself for bed. His walker was placed nearby, should he need it. Lying on his side beneath the cool covers, he slipped a hand under the soft pillow, and his gaze settled on his red tartan slippers.

All gone, he thought. *All of those I love, gone.*

What was it he needed to remember about today? There was something that he was to do. Weary from living, he hugged the pillow while he waited for sleep to help him get through another night.

Special Delivery

Linda poured the boiling water over the teabag. Small red roses dotted her favourite ceramic cup with the dainty handle. This was her secret joy – real fine bone china. Most people used mugs with stupid slogans on them or, like at work, ugly-coloured plain ones. She stuck to drinking water when working. Home was for enjoying her tea in the delicate teacup.

Linda loved the china set she had bought in a charity shop six months ago. She relished placing the matching milk jug and sugar bowl on her rectangular oak tray. It was decorated with a hand-embroidered tray cloth which her mother had made for her.

A small round coffee table took pride of place by her two-seater sofa. She sat there and enjoyed this simple tea ritual most evenings.

Tonight, she was tired. The day had been busy at the nursing home. Some of the residents at Butterfly Gardens had been grumpy and awkward to deal with. It only took one to start off, be in a cranky mood, and then like wildfire, others would decide to be the same. She often joked to her boyfriend, Brian that sometimes it was like dealing with young children in a crèche.

Tonight, Brian was away on an overnight delivery. His work took him on long-haul truck drives across Europe, often away for up to four nights. There could be even longer hours absent from Linda, if others were out sick, as he would have to cover their deliveries and pickups.

The first night they met, Linda had been out with her workmate, Katie, in the pub. The two young women had been sitting near the window when he'd asked her about the empty seat next to her. His Bradley Cooper blue eyes had immediately drawn her in, and she could not stop admiring him. When later she was squeezing by him to leave, he apologised for being in her way. "Safe home," he'd called after her, as she and Katie disappeared off into the night. The next week, Brian had been there again, and Linda had popped over to say hello.

Now, 18 months later, they were saving for a flat together. Her present one was too small for two people, no matter how much they loved each other. With his job taking him away for nights, Brian preferred to live with his parents' rather than rent a place where he would rarely stay. So, buying their own home was an important decision for the young couple.

***

"It's going to take forever to get a place." Brian threw the laptop on the bed where he was sitting. He had been checking their account online. A friend at work had told him about a new block of flats being built and suggested Brian should get his deposit down as soon as he could.

"How short are we?" Linda snuggled up to him and wrapped her arms around his waist. She didn't like his cross moods. But she was good at distracting him, and placed a soft kiss on his neck.

"About 30 grand." He kissed the top of her head then untangled himself from her hug and got up.

"But we're saving as hard as we can," she said. "I've asked about more shifts, but there's nothing extra. I could look at getting some part-time work as well as my job."

Brian grabbed a can of beer and cranked it open, then sat back down.

"You're working long hours as it is, honey. I'll see if I can get some extra hours instead." He gulped the cold drink and ran his fingers through his spiked hair.

Linda pushed over to him and sat on his lap. "But if you take extra deliveries, we'll never see each other." She sighed and snuggled into his warm chest.

***

It wasn't fair, Linda complained to her workmates in their canteen at break-time. There was no hope for young couples like her and Brian to get onto the property ladder. They wanted to buy their own place, not pay rent forever and never own anything.

Some of her colleagues agreed, sharing their own horror stories about searching for a place to buy. A few said that of course if all the immigrants that were coming here to live stayed away, there would be more housing available. The politicians were only interested in helping them and not their own people. Many heads nodded at this statement, agreeing that charity began at home and not taking on other countries' problems.

"I'm not saying that," Linda butted in. "The deposit expected by the mortgage companies is too high. It's got nothing to do with helping refugees or asylum seekers. Look at what they are fleeing from. Anyway, I know it doesn't help the housing situation but…"

Her words met with a few grunts and dismissals. She got up to leave, but the chat flowed, with those at the table continuing to solve the world's refugee problem. As she washed her hands before going back to check on the residents in her care, she noticed Katie seated by the wall, fear filling her friend's eyes.

A laugh from the group at the table caught Linda's attention. She looked again at Katie and smiled. But Katie did not smile back.

Were they including her in their anger about foreigners? Katie was from the Philippines, after all. She had come here for work to help her parents back home. Surely those chatting did not believe this injustice about housing was the fault of people looking to better themselves and help their families. A shiver swam through Linda; this was a side to her workmates she had not picked up on before. Outside of work yes, but not here.

***

"It won't be forever. Just an extra three deliveries a month. I'm lucky to get it. I'm going to meet them on Friday for a few drinks, just to mix and chat with the other drivers." Brian shared his news with Linda, and she beamed at the thought of their savings growing and the ability to buy their new home become a real possibility.

"How did they find you? This company, I mean. What about your present employers? Are they not annoyed with you working for two companies? Can you even do that?"

"It's on my time off. Not two or three nights; just the one night driving. Simple, really, I pick up the cargo in Scotland and deliver it somewhere down south in England, and I'm home to Dublin on the next ferry." He stood, hands on his hips, and stared at his girlfriend.

Linda saw a slight frown on his handsome forehead.

"But why don't drivers from over there, in the UK do it, if it's just going from north to south?" She couldn't help feeling a little anxious.

"Because of some law about hours they drive, everything is logged. But this company gets around that because of the way or place it's registered. Anyway, does it matter?" His frown had turned into a scowl. "I'm getting serious money to do three deliveries a month and not worry about form-filling. Just collect and deliver. Simple."

Grabbing his jacket, he shrugged it on. He didn't like her questions. If she knew it was Larry who had put the work his way, she would be furious. She hated Larry. He was trouble, she said.

Larry had done a stint or two in prison for smuggling cigarettes and alcohol. When Brian had bumped into the criminal hanging around the depot looking for drivers, he decided the money was too good to turn down.

"When do you start?" asked Linda.

"This Saturday, so I won't see you for a while, babe, but I'm doing this for us. That's what you need to remember. Then, once we have our deposit, I can stick with my old job. Give me a hug, Lin. You know I love you."

She nodded and kissed him. He caressed her tenderly, yet his touch did not reassure her. A nausea gurgled in her stomach, and when he left, she curled up on the sofa, hugging her knees to her chest.

***

The following morning at work, Linda sought out Katie. They had been friends since Linda started at the nursing home, and both liked the same films. She enjoyed having Katie around to her flat when Brian was away on long-haul trips.

"Hey there, glad I found you. Do anything exciting last night?" Linda met her in the communal area for the residents. The room was being set up for Bingo.

"No, nothing, just collected some books from the library. What about you?" Katie busied herself putting chairs in a circle.

"Brian is off on extra deliveries, but not long haul, just short ones. He said it will help with our savings."

"That is good." Katie smiled.

"About yesterday, Katie. I didn't mean anything. I was speaking about the banks. You weren't hurt by any of it?" Linda fiddled with the chairs, avoiding the other care worker's stare. After a few moments, she looked at Katie.

"Linda, the others… it scared me to hear them talk that way. I didn't realise they felt so strongly. Do they speak about me?"

"Really? Nothing to be scared of. Look, ignore them. They shout louder than they think," Linda muttered as she smoothed down her tunic, side-stepping Katie's question.

Katie sighed. "Have you seen Alex this morning?" she enquired, as she picked up a chair and continued finishing the room for bingo. Linda stopped putting out large jugs of water on the tables.

"No. Why? I like Alex."

"I thought he was a bit unsettled when I helped him yesterday. Spoke about it being his wedding day." The two women surveyed their completed work.

"I will keep an eye on him and let you know if I think there's anything unusual in his behaviour today." Linda offered, happy that all appeared well between her and Katie.

***

Brian: *Hey, Babe, two runs down and it was a doddle.*

They were going to pay him cash, too, as it was easier than setting him up within the English tax system, he told her.

Linda's unease surfaced once more. It was strange dealings, and she texted Brian back, asking him to reconsider.

Brian: *Four months will see us with enough for our deposit. Think of the bigger picture, Linda. Four months, that's all.*

***

Linda and Katie were out for a late lunch. They were both on nights, so had made plans to meet before their shift started that evening.

"Did you see the photo of the little child drowned after travelling on a life raft? So terrible and sad," Linda asked, while she shook some salt onto her salad.

"Shocking," Katie replied. "The thugs who take their money and promise those desperate people new lives are evil. How terrifying it must be. Your family's life in danger like that, and setting out to sea on a small craft."

"Oh Katie, the world is cruel. How can they do that and sleep at night? Imagine smuggling people. There are some awful stories in the news." Linda paused, her fork mid-air, as she shook her head.

"People can be selfish. But what saddens me is that there are others who believe it would never happen where they live."

"Are you saying it happens here? People mistreating others because of where they are from?" Linda stopped eating and went to pick up her glass of water.

"Yes, and it has to me. People jump me in queues, push me out of the way. Some have spat at me. Look how the others at work spoke about foreigners. That surprised me… and concerned me." Katie watched her friend's colour change; she looked pale. Surely, Linda wasn't so naïve as to be shocked by Katie's words?

***

Linda got up early and pulled the curtains back. She looked upwards; the clouds were like padded footprints of a kitten playing in the vast blue sky. It was a special day. She and Brian had managed it! They had their deposit, and she was meeting him in exactly two hours.

Together, they held hands as Brian pushed the door open for his girlfriend to step through. The auctioneer greeted them and offered coffee or tea. They were really doing this; they were buying their own apartment. Linda watched the confident way Brian signed the contract, his signature sweeping beneath her tidy handwriting. She loved him with everything she had. He turned and smiled at her. They were homeowners, and the trio were shaking hands and laughing.

Four months passed, when Brian signed up for another four with Larry. He told Linda that the contract had been extended and that he would get a bonus if he remained to help them out. She couldn't really argue when their bank balance was healthy and growing. She occupied her time with picking out colours and materials, putting together mood boards for each room, and pinning her ideas to those.

"I handed in my notice with my old job." Brian paused, and when Linda didn't reply, he continued, "I'm going to go full-time with this new company." He held his hands up before her, stopping her from speaking. "Before you jump down my throat, they have arranged a run from Belfast through Dublin to England. I won't be away long-haul any more. It makes sense, Lin. I'll be working from Ireland and coming home the night after. A short trip across the Irish Sea."

"You've made your mind up. Why bother with what I think," she snapped, and went to put the kettle on.

"It's good money and our savings are growing. I thought you'd be pleased. I've missed you, Lin." He watched her make a pot of tea and get out those flimsy tea cups he always feared he'd break when holding one.

"What is it they ship? What stock do they carry?" Her anger had cooled. She couldn't argue when he mentioned their savings. It was all for them and their future.

"Why the sudden interest in what the containers hold?" He scratched his head.

"If my boyfriend is going to be working in a new job, I'd like to know about it." Her smile told him she was giving him the okay.

"Instead of your boyfriend, what if you called him your fiancé?" Brian dropped to one knee and presented a red velvet box.

She screamed, jumped, and dropped her china cup. Splinters went flying and hot tea splashed in the air.

***

Linda and Katie discussed wedding dresses and flowers. When Katie asked who Brian worked for and if Linda had met his co-workers, she brushed it off. The bride-to-be knew very little about the company, only it had provided her with their new home, and Brian was around a lot more than he'd been before. She had pushed down any doubts that threatened to ruin her future, but Katie's questions raised them up again.

Linda's happiness rubbed off on Katie, and she noticed that her friend was not so homesick now. One of the male nurses had started flirting with Katie, and she liked him. She and Linda spoke of going on double-dates next time Brian was home.

The young women went about their chores, with Linda being congratulated on her engagement.

While the residents were being served their dinner, a buzz of whispers started to build amongst the staff. Ripples and snippets of conversations gathered in corners, some of the residents were asking what was happening. The atmosphere in the home was charged. Why were the staff gasping and shaking their heads at words others shared with them? People looked over their shoulders, checking who was around before they spoke.

Katie walked into the sitting room to help settle the residents to watch some evening television. Linda followed, checking on her charges and chatting and laughing as the end of her shift neared. She was going home to curl up with her tea and watch a film. Brian would be phoning her later.

"Scum! Hope they rot in hell, playing with those poor peoples' lives," a resident shouted.

Linda turned to see some staff gathered around the large television screen showing the evening news. She moved closer, with Katie near her. On the screen was a large grey container surrounded by police, blue lights flashing, and media crews behind the police tape. It had come through the ferry to England. Inside were 40 people, starved and sick; as yet it was unclear whether there were any fatalities. The container had been delivered that morning. One of the port workers noticed the seal had been damaged and alerted the authorities. Police had been investigating this company for some time, and they believed the company was a front for a northern European people-trafficking gang.

The lorry driver's photo flashed across the screen. The reporter on telly said the driver admitted to knowing what the cargo he transported was. At present, he was in custody at a nearby police station. Katie gasped when she saw Brian's face staring out at her.

Linda, who stood beside her, remained silent. She would know those blue eyes anywhere. Her heart pulsed in her chest, and a pain shot through it. She struggled for air and put her hands out to grab support. The chair back she caught toppled and fell to the floor.

Hey, Paddy

I asked Jimmy what he had had for breakfast. Jimmy said, "CocoPops, why?"

"No why," I said, "just wondering."

I asked my other friend, Oran, "Do you like soccer?"

"Of course," he said, "everyone loves soccer."

Then I asked my dad. "Am I different?"

My dad's eyes clouded over, and for a quick second he glanced away before he answered me. "What do you mean, different?"

"In school, some of the kids shout at me. Say I'm not from here, and I should go home."

My dad said not to listen to them; children often said silly things. He smiled at me then, but I knew when my dad was worried. His face changed, his mouth pretended to smile, but his eyes wanted to cry. He looked like that now. I knew my father was not able to answer my question; or maybe he could, but he didn't want to upset me.

I tried not to think about the name-calling and the jokes which I mostly didn't understand. My sister, Chloe, who was four years older than me, didn't seem to have any problems with school or friends since we'd moved here. Maybe girls were different; maybe being 13 was easier.

Monday mornings were the worst. I walked with my head down, and when I'd hear them calling my name, I'd walk faster. But they would run after me and punch me in the back, and I would fall forward. My knees were always bruised. Sometimes they pulled my coat by the hood, and I choked, as it was hard to breathe. Oran and Jimmy would yell at them to leave me alone. But it didn't matter. They would get shoved around, too, for helping me. After that, they stayed quiet when it happened.

Waiting for the bus, certain lads, the bigger fellas, would mock the way I talked, said I sounded like a caveman. Had they not heard an Irish accent before?

"Have you cabbages in your school bag? Ignorant and stupid, all of ye, with ye're Holy Marys and leprechauns. Hey, Paddy, are you still growing the spuds? You got hairy pigs in your garden?" Then one of the lads would catch the strap of my backpack and pull it just as I was going to step down the bus aisle, and I would be jerked back.

The other passengers would shout and tell me to be careful, and push me if I fell up against them. The shouting would have the driver telling me, "Behave, and move along down the bus!" But it wasn't my fault.

"Hey, your dad's in the IRA, he blows up people," they would say, then they would spit at me, point their hands like a gun and go, "Bang!"

I tried not to cry. My dad wasn't in any gang. Mam hugged me after I asked her what the IRA was. She said she was sorry she couldn't take me to school herself, but she was working now. Things were more expensive over here, but soon they would have money saved and enough to buy a house back in Callyhilll. We wouldn't be here forever.

Mam was a little sad leaving Ireland, but she kept saying we would go back once Dad and her were back on their feet and things had improved back home. It certainly was better than when we'd lived in County Cork. Over there, Dad had no job. The factory had closed down, and after a long time when he couldn't find any work, my parents kept worrying about money. It was not easy to make ends meet.

I would sit on the stairs and listen to them talk. I heard stories about Dad's friends drinking too much because they'd nothing else to do during the day other than going to the pub. Mam said if Dad ever thought he could do that, then he was on his own. She said she'd take us – me and Chloe – and go live with her sister. He'd never see us again.

Dad said he wasn't stupid; he loved us and Mam. Then Mam said she knew that, and she was just worried and tired of not having money. Then they were talking about leaving Ireland, going to relations in England. I didn't want to leave my friends, but I didn't say that to Mam and Dad, because then they'd know I had been listening to their conversations. Children aren't supposed to listen to grown-up stuff. Dad said they'd wait about leaving for another while before they'd contact our cousins.

Mam tried to get work, but all the foreigners had taken the jobs in the supermarkets and cleaning offices. Even in the fast-food places, there weren't any jobs. Our local chipper didn't have any Irish working there now.

"It's a disgrace how they can come into our country and do that," Mam and her friends said when they sat in the kitchen having their tea in the mornings.

It was during one of the morning get-togethers that Dad burst into the kitchen and said, "Theresa, we're leaving." He was all excited. His cousin had got him an interview in the factory where he worked in Birmingham.

The other mothers went all quiet and looked at Mam. But she was smiling. She said Dad was great to look after his family.

I think my sister was the only one happy – oh, and Mam a little bit. Maybe girls like moving to different places. Dad's cousin in Birmingham wasn't married and didn't have children. That was a shame, Mam said, because we would have had someone to play with and be friends with in school.

My school in Birmingham was huge, and there were hundreds of children. I don't know why they laughed at my accent, because I couldn't understand them either. One of the boys called me Paddy and the others laughed, but I told them that was my name. I explained it was another way to say Pádraig, and then he said I was being smart.

"Do you think you're cleverer than us? Ye Paddies are only good at drinking and fighting." Then he punched me in the stomach, and I fell down. When I got up and went to walk away, I was tripped and fell again.

"Look, he's drunk like his Da, can't walk, ha." I didn't tell Mam or Dad, because I knew Dad wasn't happy in England either.

"It's not very friendly like home. Everyone here just does their job and says nothing. No-one talks to you," he told Mam one evening when they were sitting in the new kitchen having a talk. Mam said nothing, but I could see her head nodding.

Jimmy and Oran lived two streets away from me. They were born here.

"My grandad's from Ireland," Jimmy said. "He's always talking about the home place. He starts singing these songs about England taking over Ireland, when he's been drinking whiskey. He catches my hand and says, 'Don't ever forget where you're from; always remember your roots'." Jimmy pretended to be old when he said this, shaking his head and hands, and walking slowly. Oran and I laughed at him. Jimmy was funny.

Oran said he wasn't Irish at all. His parents were from Birmingham, and his grandad and grandma owned a market-stall in the big shopping centre, The Bullring. He likes it here.

I said I liked it here, too, when I wasn't being picked on. I told them about the small town where I'd lived in Ireland. We didn't have a swimming pool or a cinema, and it could be boring during the summer. At least in Birmingham you had pools and big shopping centres and always somewhere to go. In Ireland, I said, there weren't many people either, or noise. But Birmingham had lots of people everywhere you went. And it was very noisy.

"Is all Ireland like your town?" Oran asked.

I nodded. I guess it was, as I'd never heard people say it was noisy. I wasn't able to sleep when we came to Birmingham at the start. The sirens and cars never stopped on our street here.

"That's because we live near a hospital," Jimmy said. "Our street is noisy, too."

***

During the summer holidays, Mam, Chloe, and I went back to visit our family in Ireland. It felt strange to be there. We stayed with Mam's sister, and our cousins said we had funny accents, that we said some words like Irish people and some like English people. I just shrugged my shoulders and said no more. I didn't like it when they said that.

I was the same as them, but they said I wasn't Irish any more now that I was living in England. But I wasn't English either. I had no place where I was from now. I felt lonely when I thought that. Their mam, my aunty, called us the English cousins now, and a bad pain would cut my stomach when she said it.

The town was very quiet, and I missed the sirens when I went to bed. I wanted Indian food, too, not just burger and chips and battered sausages from the chipper. My cousins said Indian food was "Yuck", but they had never tasted it. All we did was play soccer and hurling during the day. In Birmingham you could go to the libraries and big parks.

But I liked it when people said to me, "Oh, you're Theresa's boy. Are you here on holidays? How's your dad?" They remembered who I was. So maybe I was still more Irish than English.

When we got back to Birmingham, I told Dad that people had asked about him. He smiled at this – a real happy smile. His eyes smiled, too.

"It feels good not to be forgotten," he said.

***

In September, when we returned to school, it wasn't all bad. The bully boys took less notice of my accent now, but they still pulled my hair, threw stones, and shouted, "Score!" when a stone hit me. If they were behind me in a queue, they would shove chewed chewing gum into my hair and then rub it in. I told Mam that it came from the bus seats, as people stuck their gum on the headrests. Jimmy and Oran said I had lost my Irish way of speaking, but I didn't mind that.

Mam was delighted when her boss said she was going to be in charge of the girls on the checkouts at her work. She and Dad drank wine that night to celebrate.

"Life is getting better for sure. Well done, honey, on your promotion," he said, and he kissed her. We were all laughing and had Indian takeaway for dinner to celebrate with the wine.

Mam texted her friends back home to tell them. They all were happy for her and said that would never happen in Ireland. She had been right to leave. She hugged Dad and told him how clever he was for bringing us to Birmingham.

The factory where Dad worked was getting bigger. There were more jobs, and he told his old friends in Callyhill about it. But they said things were picking up in Ireland now and that they were happier to stay there. Plus, this talk of England leaving the EU had been on the news, and they thought it was better not to go.

Mam and Dad were talking in the kitchen, and I was listening on the stairs. They said England wouldn't leave Europe, as it was one of the big players. Anyway, they had good wages now, and we children were happy here, so they wouldn't think about it until the government in London said something.

I asked Jimmy and Oran about it. They said that their parents were talking about it, too, but did I see the new film about Star Wars was coming out later? We all love Star Wars. We said we would go together on a Saturday and see it. The new film, *Episode VIII – The Force Awakens*, has everyone talking about it in school.

Chloe is only interested in her fake tan. Mam said she had all our towels ruined. They have orange bits all over them.

***

My cousins in Cork came over for a week after Christmas. I wanted to bring them to the public leisure centre and show them all the huge shops, so I texted them to bring lots of money.

My aunty said she could never get used to the noise on our street and all the people rushing around, no-one smiling. Mam was a bit annoyed and said, "Well, people keep to themselves here, they don't interfere in others' business."

My cousins loved the swimming pool and the sauna. The nearest one to them was over 40 miles away. There was one closer, but that was in a hotel and was very expensive to join.

Jimmy and Oran called to say hello. My cousins said it was hard to understand them, but we all sat and watched the football on telly. The cousins even liked the curry Mam bought from the Indian place for dinner.

Mam and Aunty were in the kitchen, and when I went to get cola and crisps for us watching the match, I heard my aunt giving out. "You give them too much freedom, Theresa. Sure, Pádraig is what, ten now, and he goes to the swimming pool alone by bus? Anything could happen."

"He is with his friends," Mam said. "All the children here get the bus to go places. I am working, you know. I can't be everywhere. And sure, in the cities at home in Ireland, don't they do the same? It's not any different to here."

They went quiet when I walked in, and Mam ruffled my hair and smiled. I looked at my aunty and she looked away. Later that evening, she and Mam had another fight. Aunty was trying to get Mam to come back to Ireland.

I pretended to get a bucket of coal outside for the fire, and Mam smiled at me when I went through the kitchen. I gave my aunty a dirty look; she shouldn't be upsetting my mam. On the way back, I stayed outside the back door and listened.

"Things have improved. It's changed. This place is not where Pádraig and Chloe should be. My heart would be in my mouth every time they'd go out with their friends. God knows what they get up to or see or meet," my aunt said in a scary way.

"Listen, don't tell me Ireland is a pot of gold all of a sudden. We struggled when Mick lost his job. I couldn't get work. We would have been homeless if it kept going the way it was, and I hear on the news that those figures for the homeless are rising. Our children would probably have to leave after school anyway. At least I don't hear of anyone leaving over here. What have we to go back for? Mick got a job here when he couldn't at home. The children have settled, and I'm enjoying my work. If you can match that, then I'll think about going back." Mam banged her hand on the table.

I went in then and walked slowly past them. My aunty said I was a good lad to keep the fire on, but I didn't smile at her. I just looked at Mam. "You alright, Mam?" I asked, and she nodded.

When my cousins and aunty had gone home, I asked Chloe if she liked living in Birmingham. She said it was okay. I asked her if she'd like to go back to live in our small old town, and she said she wouldn't mind. She missed a few of her friends still. She asked me why I was asking, and I told her about Mam and our aunty talking. She asked what I thought about going back, and I told her I didn't want to. She was surprised at that, because her eyes opened wide, and she shook her head.

***

Dad and Mam are wondering what to do. The talk about England leaving Europe is on all the news now. Brexit, it's called. People are saying all those that are not from Britain should be sent home. There've been various attacks on innocent people walking home from work or out shopping.

Jimmy and Oran are okay; they were born here. But I'm getting a bit scared about it, and I asked Dad what we would do if they threw us out of England.

"They won't do that, Pádraig. Ireland and England have a special relationship. Sure, we built this country for them. Don't worry."

I told my friends what my dad said, and they were delighted. I was happy, too, as we would now be friends forever. Chloe asked how I could say that; what about my friends in Ireland that I left behind? I told her they were not my friends any more. They had said I didn't sound Irish during the holiday to Cork, and that had annoyed me. Anyway, I had Jimmy and Oran now, and we were going to travel the world together and have great fun when we finished school. They didn't mind what way I talked; they were real friends.

Chloe said she wished she was like me. I told her to stop putting on that fake tan and she would be like me then.

My friends and I went to the shopping centre today to get a present for Jimmy's dad. He was 50, and they were having a party for him. While we were in the shop, we heard a lot of shouting. Outside on the mall, several older boys were fighting, hitting each other with fists, then we heard a kind of scream or groan and there was blood.

It was on the TV news that night. Dad and Mam said it was shocking that people were like that. I asked, like what? "Fighting because people were different to them," they said.

In bed that night, I remembered being different when I came here. Now I'm worried I will be stabbed or attacked. I texted Jimmy and Oran and told them I was scared. Jimmy said I would be okay. No-one would attack me because I sounded like them now, he said, and I was the same colour.

Oran said he was worried because he wasn't the same colour. But Jimmy and I said we would protect him. We said we were like the three musketeers, so it would all be okay.

Our street got busier with sirens, and I asked Mam if that was because people were fighting each other like in the shopping centre. She said no, it was just busy, that's all. But I wasn't allowed go to The Bullring without Mam or Dad any more. So, Jimmy and Oran and I went to a green area near Jimmy's house and played football.

Dad came home early from work a few times. One dinnertime, he told Mam that the orders for the factory were slowing down after the stupid people had voted yes to leave the EU. Now people were worried what would happen if the other countries didn't want the stuff Dad's factory made.

Chloe said she has a new boyfriend, and she's in love. Mam's fighting with her about her short skirts and that she looks cheap. Mam said maybe our aunty was right, it was hard to keep an eye on your children over here.

Dad is home early again today. He closed the door very quietly, so we hardly heard him come in. I watched Mam watching Dad. She threw the tea-towel down on the counter and went to put the kettle on, while Dad rubbed his face with his hands and sat down hard on his chair by the window. Then he shook his head like a dog does when it's wet. I never saw him do that before. He looks… tired… old, maybe. Yeah, old and… sad. Then Mam closed the kitchen door.

At dinnertime, he said he had news and that we had decisions to make. He mumbled that the factory mightn't need him every day. Mam looked frightened. Chloe kept looking at her phone, texting her boyfriend. I kept looking at Dad. His eyes weren't smiling.

Enough is Enough

Tonight, was not about roadways or education. Tonight's meeting was to take action and control, swift and decisive, no ifs or buts. This was how Councillor Sheila Nugent did things. A quick glance in the mirror to check her lipstick and run a comb through her grey permed hair, and she was good to go.

The room was well heated for the late wintry weather, with chairs surrounding the white plastic top table. Refreshments were placed to the side of the room for the after-meeting catch-up.

Sheila held the poster by its top corners with her thumbs and forefingers. It was clear in its message, the words in black stood out against the pale grey background. Clear and simple. *The world was changing, and it wasn't nice*, she noted to herself. *Everyone seemed to have rights, yet no-one had responsibilities. It was time to call a halt.*

Sheila was not Councillor of Callyhill to look pretty in photographs. She had been voted in to protect this town, and promote it, too. Her campaign for services for the schools and the need for financial funding for other local matters had been successful. More and more were choosing to live in her town. Its proximity to the city was a major driving force for this, and the promise of a new motorway added to the attraction.

"Sheila. Always the first one here, fair play to you." Teddy hung his coat up on the wall hooks and shook himself, while clapping his hands for warmth. The outside chill had followed him in.

"Ah, Teddy. Well, I like to lead by example." Sheila smiled at her friend who was the vice-chairperson of the committee. The two of them had grown up near each other and remained loyal to the town, never leaving it in all their years.

"You look grand as always." He popped on a kettle and brewed a pot of tea, desperate for a warm drink. Gesturing to Sheila if she wanted a tea, she nodded in reply. He didn't need to ask how she took it; a drop of milk and two sugars.

The Councillor sometimes wondered if she hadn't married her late husband, whether things might have developed between her and Teddy. The door opening, and the rush of cold again blowing in, took her from her thoughts.

A bundle of posters was placed in the centre of the table as everyone took their seats. All the committee members were present, knowing it was an important meeting. Sheila told them they required a united front if the campaign was to be successful, and within two hours, it was agreed – Teddy being the only one to express a different voice. Callyhill would oppose the turning of the empty convent into housing more refugees. They would not support it, and Sheila, their Councillor, would lead the charge.

Driving home, her heart was troubled. Although delighted with the result of the meeting, not having Teddy one hundred percent behind her niggled. She noticed he hadn't waited around after the agenda was over, but slipped away quietly.

Watching the news, she settled down with a small sherry. It was all about those poor people drifting across seas on small boats. Trouble everywhere. But *enough was enough*; her town couldn't take any more foreigners. Her thoughts returned to the heated exchange between her and Ted earlier.

"It is not the fault of those people seeking a new home, we should be helping them," Ted insisted.

"Help them? Our town is crawling with foreigners, we haven't got the room, Ted." Some of those present murmured in agreement.

"Sheila, are we not honour-bound morally to help?"

"What about our own? We all have children that will need jobs, houses, and if they can't avail of that, then they will have to leave. Why, old Jimmy Jones has none of his family left here all abroad, nothing available, as indeed my own two boys, and I wonder why that is?"

"I think you are taking the wrong approach is all I'm saying. As our Councillor, should you not be leading the way in helping others?"

"As your Councillor, Ted, it is my duty to protect our town and right now since our new residents have arrived, we are seeing anti-social activity on our streets on the increase and not a word of English to be heard as you walk our Main Street."

"You cannot blame rising crime on people who have come here seeking out a new life."

"Not all of it, no, but have you not seen the social media videos, these people who don't fit in with our lifestyle and customs? They think it's okay to harass young women at night after closing time and then young fellas fighting amongst themselves during the day. What about protecting our good name in tourism? Tourists enhance our economy, our town benefits from tourists visiting and that is what I intend to protect. Our good name, Ted, plain and simple."

"Sheila, I cannot support this attitude. It's a dangerous opinion you're putting out there. People look to people in your position for guidance, not to hear the rants of... of..."

"Say it, Ted! Racially prejudiced – discriminatory - bigoted? I'm not sorry that I feel so strongly about our town being over-run with asylum seekers, refugees, or whatever name they are hiding beneath now. I am watching out for our future generations."

She hated disagreeing with her friend, but he was wrong on this occasion.

Her eyes gazed upon the photo of her boys that looked down on her from the marble mantelpiece. Now in their thirties, she wished they lived closer, not a long plane journey away. A lump gathered in her throat. Any potential grandchildren would be living away from her, and she would miss them growing up. Living their lives through photographs.

If only someone had stood up to those foreigners, or was it non-nationals you must call them now? It kept changing, Sheila thought. *They had saturated the country, putting extra strain on all resources, leaving little if nothing for our own. Yes, enough was enough.* She was sure that was the reason her boys had left after college in search of work.

***

The phone ringing woke Sheila from her sleep the next morning. It was seven forty-five.

"Hello, Sheila speaking," she replied groggily, then listened to a tirade of abuse from someone she did not know. Fully awake now, she clicked off the mobile.

She had known there would be a backlash for the decision taken last night, but word was definitely out now. Two of the men had offered to nail up the posters around the town after the meeting. The small placards clearly stated their message:

Callyhill Says No to Convent Refugee Camp.

It was the beginning of the battle, yet Sheila was prepared.

***

The tree-lined avenue where Sheila lived was shaking to the cry of an angry wind. She held onto her scarf with tight fists while leaning into the strong gale, her shopping bag swinging on her arm. The short walk to her neighbouring shops was a ritual at the start of each day.

"Well, Sheila, you've opened a right can of worms this time." The butcher shook his head as he got her usual order of four rashers, six sausages, and a half each of black and white puddings.

"I take it you don't agree." She retrieved her purse from her navy bag.

"I do. And I don't." He wrapped the meat in white paper and placed the parcel into a plastic bag. "The people coming to live need help; our help. They're not coming for a holiday, and yeah, I know it seems they're everywhere, but they need our support."

"Hmm… well you can have your opinion, but I believe the vacant convent could be put to better use." Sheila left the butchers feeling miffed, but then reassured herself that he would take that view. After all, he had Brazilians employed in his meat factory and was always saying what good hardworking people they were.

***

Her phone hopped with calls and text messages. Any numbers she didn't recognise, she dismissed. It was all overwhelming. Being Councillor was difficult work, but she had made a promise to serve the people and that is what she would do. By 12 that day, the media had come to her town. There would be no avoiding them.

Where was Teddy? She had meant to phone him, but would do it now. His phone went straight to voicemail; he was probably fending off calls, too. He had always been a good friend, loyal all through the years, supportive when her husband died, and the boys left after college.

Her appointment at the dentist could not be put off, and she decided if she had to face people she may as well get it over with. Sheila parked her car and looked around before getting out. People in the waiting room raised their heads as she entered, some looked away in disgust, yet no-one challenged her. A few curt grunts and nods was all she got. Even the dentist was quiet. She left happy but sore.

"Excuse me, Councillor Nugent. Richard from CWL Radio, can we ask: are you in agreement with what these posters all over the town are saying? Have you given this decision your backing, and if yes, why so?" The young man with his microphone stood close to her as she turned away from her car door.

"Good afternoon," she answered calmly. "Yes, I am in agreement with the stand Callyhill is taking against this latest measure by those in Europe to swamp our town with more... more... people than we can cater for."

"But in the past you have always said Callyhill is a welcoming town. You pride yourself in all the opportunities that it has to offer. Are you saying now that those opportunities are only available for locals?" He shifted closer to her.

"I still pride myself on our town. But enough is enough; we just don't have the facilities. I'm not saying these people should not receive help, but it should be in a place that can offer it to them better than we can. Is that so hard to understand?"

"Councillor, are you sure in saying everyone in Callyhill agrees with you?"

She shook her head. "I'm not that silly. Of course, some will not agree, but once they see the sense behind my town's decision, they will change their minds, I should think."

The reporter's eyes widened at the word *my,* then he smiled broadly and clicked off his microphone. He turned without a goodbye and walked smartly away.

***

Teddy sat in the café. He didn't like this one bit. Sheila had surprised him with her actions. *How could he be a part of something he didn't agree with? Or was it he who was wrong? Were people fed up with sharing our villages, towns, cities? The convent was vacant; why not use it for good?* He sipped his coffee, but it had lost its flavour. Pulling his cap on and buttoning up his coat, he left the warmth and headed out into the strong gales. Teddy needed to do a few chores before he went home. What to do with Sheila was troubling him. He was worried she had tackled something that could destroy her. She had done well for the town; it would be a shame for that to be forgotten. He would call over to her in the morning.

***

The rain lashed down as the days passed, the local river swelling and threatening to spill over. Teddy hoped this would divert attention from the convent problem. He tried phoning Sheila, but it was ringing out or engaged. There would be nothing for it but to visit. He knocked on the door and didn't realise he held his breath until his friend opened it.

"Ted! Come in."

"I've been ringing you. How are you?" he said, as he went about taking off his coat, the hospitality of the house welcome.

"I don't know where to start, Ted," she admitted wearily. "I'm in the wars since our meeting."

"I saw; either the papers or the radio are quoting you. But I did warn you, Sheila." He followed her to the sitting room.

"I still believe what I did was right," she replied defiantly. "We can't cope with what we have, and I really can't make out why I'm the bad guy. I'm only saying what others are thinking."

"Not all of us."

"Will you stop? Our own are leaving because of letting in everyone who says they're fleeing war, fear, and whatever other excuse they shout about. It has to stop. They know they have it good; that's why they are sneaking in. Was there not a report a few weeks back about how some asylum seekers didn't have correct papers to enter and yet got through? Now don't tell me I'm wrong."

"Look, Sheila, I didn't come for an argument. I came to check on you. But you seem to be doing fine." He hadn't even sat on his usual spot on the floral sofa.

"Sorry, Teddy. I'll go put the kettle on." Sheila brought in a tray filled with a pot of tea, two china cups, and some bourbon biscuits – his favourite – on a matching china plate. They drank in silence and munched on the biscuits while listening to the torrential rain cleaning the streets.

"Has anyone from the council been in touch about the river?" he asked eventually. "It's pretty swollen." The rain lashed the window, strengthening the apprehension of his words.

"No. To be honest, it's the least of my problems, but thanks for telling me. I'll give Pat a ring."

"Would you not let the convent issue go, Sheila?"

Her stare told him the answer. Her lips tightened into a narrow line, and she drew in a breath, releasing it slowly. "Ted. Not again." Her smile was weak.

This issue was definitely stressing their friendship. His broad shoulders leant against the sofa, his right hand lying on the armrest, the rose-pink cushion from the corner tossed to the other side.

***

The note fell silently in the letterbox. It wasn't until Sheila was going out for her daily walk that she spotted it. No envelope, just a sheet of folded paper.

STOP your protest now or YOU will be sorry

Sheila read the words again. *Stupid nonsense.* She wrapped her scarf snugly inside her coat and threw the note on the hallway side table. *Why didn't people understand she was watching out for them, their children, their future?* These do-gooders were taking over and not thinking about the consequence of their actions. It was all fine and good to be shouting about helping others, but the town did not have the facilities, the government department hadn't notified them, no discussion about anything had taken place. And she was supposed to say 'yes' to all of this?

Her thoughts flitted to her sons. How she missed them. They should be here, they should have had the choice of living here, but no.

She walked down towards the river path. The rain had stopped, so that was a bonus. The angry waters rushed through under the bridge, but fears of flooding were low, she noted. Typical Teddy, always worrying. Her walk took her along the street by the former convent, and she stopped and admired the strong, decorative building. It stood proud upon a slight hill, its structure appealing. What a lovely hotel or hostel it would make. Draw in the tourists, money for the town to continue developing. Stupid using it for individuals who came from God knows where and why. She straightened her back and walked on, determined it would not happen on her watch.

The sight of her curtains blowing out through the broken window had Sheila rushing up her garden path. The large bricks – two of them covered in muck – lay on her sitting room floor. Ornaments had been knocked over and out of place by the strong wind that had rushed around and caused chaos through the huge hole. Papers were scattered behind the sofa, under the coffee table. Her photo, her favourite photo, lay on the marble hearth, its glass smashed, her boys' faces scratched and scarred.

***

"That's it, you are dropping your protest about the convent." Teddy held his friend in a hug. Shock still ran through her as her body trembled in his arms.

"I can't, Ted. I can't let thugs drive me out. The window is all sealed up. I'll be fine. The Gardaí have everything: the note, the rocks, everything."

"And who are you blaming this violence on? Our own people, as you like to say, or the refugees? Did you tell the Gardaí your thoughts on our local rise on crime?" He went to her sideboard and poured himself a whiskey and a sherry for her. "Sheila, I am not letting you put yourself in danger."

"Teddy, stop. It's because of this bullying by people who think they are the only ones who are right that this country has become overrun with undesirables. I am more than ever determined to play my part and stand up to them." The sherry glass was emptied in one long swallow.

Teddy remained silent. He was angry with her. He didn't understand why he had not noticed this nastiness before in Sheila. Their companionship was always a loving one but this… well, he did not know if he could continue the friendship.

"My boys were driven out because of this, this look-after-others-and-feck-our own. I'm here on my own when I should have my family around me." She sat upright and looked at the damaged photo on the mantle.

"Nonsense. Your boys left because they wanted to, and there is nothing to stop you from visiting them. It is you who made the choice not to." Teddy stood up and pulled on his coat. He looked at Sheila, still sitting down.

She remained seated. She did not look at him, her hands clutching the glass tightly. His words had cut her, as she'd expected him to understand her position. Flashes of the strained Christmas dinners when the boys had returned taunted her now.

The polite chat, the long silences, the brief stay. Her insistence they should visit her, not her travel to them. They should want to come home; this is where she was, their roots.

After Teddy left her, Sheila poured another sherry. Standing before her boarded-up window, she sipped the deep wine drink. Its flavour warmed her throat and settled her nerves. She looked around the room. It felt soiled. It felt invaded. It felt contaminated. Nobody had actually come in, but she would need to clean it from top to bottom.

***

Tonight's meeting would be one of celebration. Sheila had everything set up before the other committee members arrived. Glancing down the order of the agenda, her heart sank a little. There was only one item of news she was not looking forward to. Those who had supported her rambled in, others had resigned. A happy atmosphere tickled the air as they applauded the successful Councillor Sheila Nugent. She smiled at her colleagues and thanked them for their support; her win was their win.

Her eyes were drawn to the empty chair beside her. Teddy's resignation was next on the agenda. With a deep breath, she composed herself. She had done the right thing. It took sacrifices to stand up for what you believed in. Her boys and Teddy had made their choices. She was entitled to hers, too. Sheila pasted on a smile, looked around the room, and spoke with confidence. "Next up, a vote for a new vice-chairperson."

The Crochet Circle

The women sat in a circle around the large conference table. They could be seen through the glass wall that separated them from the rest of their local library. The room was soundproofed, and these ladies had it booked every Tuesday morning at ten o'clock for their two-hour gathering. On the table was an array of colours and textures from light to dark, thread from double to chunky. Yarn was spread out, works in progress on their laps.

Debbie looked at her companions, a blanket of concentration connecting them. Some were working furiously with the pattern repeat off by heart; a few deep in study of the leaflet containing the instructions like it was an exam; idle chit-chat for others. She lived for this group – women after her own heart, who enjoyed the feel of the yarn as it wound through their fingers and watched as the work in progress grew from a simple slip stitch to a labyrinth of trebles, doubles, and clusters.

"Did you see the news this morning? Tragedy in England, people found in a container. What a world we live in." Debbie spoke as she unravelled some mint green wool. In her mid-sixties, she had been reared with darning socks and turning shirt collars. Recycling before it became a hip thing to do.

"Dreadful altogether. The lorry driver lives not far from here. Engaged to a local girl, I believe," another replied.

"NO! He can't be! One of our own behaving like that? No, that's got to be gossip, someone exaggerating. Where did you hear it from?" Debbie put her work down and looked around the table. Silence. A darkness swept through this sacred space at the unpleasant news.

"My Jackie works with her, the one he's engaged to, up at the nursing home, Butterfly Gardens." No-one crocheted, the flow of the work stopped by the horror of it being on their doorstep.

"Time for tea, some refreshment, and then we can get back to it, I reckon," Peg offered. She was the group leader and busied herself at a nearby burco. Tea and coffee and plates of chocolate digestives, with a few scattered custard creams mixed in, were on offer. Yet no-one could eat, the magic of the group had been tarnished.

Rima, the latest member, didn't speak English very well. She sat quietly drinking her coffee. Often, her words got jumbled up, which was confusing for Debbie who had once tried to help her with the cluster stitch. Right now, Debbie noticed the girl looked like a lost child, and saw tears sliding quietly down her cheeks, unnoticed by the others.

***

Standing in the queue at the bakers, Debbie was about to order the special of the day to go: four custard slices for five euro. She spotted Rima sitting in the corner of the small café to the rear of the cake shop.

Bundling her cakes into her shopping bag, she walked towards the seated woman, who had her head down and was busy reading.

"Hello there, Rima," Debbie's greeting took the younger woman by surprise.

Rima flicked back her dark hair from her shoulders. "Hello, Debbie."

"Mind if I join you?" Debbie pulled back the empty chair across from Rima and sat, placing her shopping on the floor and her coat behind her on the chair.

"Well now, how are you?"

Rima nodded and said in a hushed tone, "Okay." She closed her book and pushed it to the side of the table.

"Oh, don't let me stop you. Read away. I wanted to rest my legs, and I spotted you. Thought I would pop over and say hello." Debbie caught the eye of a waitress and ordered a pot of tea.

Rima remained quiet.

Debbie moved on her chair, uncomfortable with the woman's silence. Maybe she'd made a mistake sitting down here, but she was just trying to be friendly. Her husband said she mustn't judge those who were new to the town until she knew their story. She had filled him in on how the group at the library was changing.

"What are you reading?" she pointed at the table. Rima's eyes followed the finger to her book.

"English." Then she picked it up and turned it to show the cover to her unexpected companion.

"Oh, *Improving your English*. Ah, that's great, you're not the best at our language, are you? Do you like the crochet group?" Debbie worked her hands as if she had a hook and ball of wool on her lap.

Rima laughed and said, "Yes, yes." Working her fingers like Debbie, she pretended to crochet.

Rima read and Debbie drank her tea. Then, as swiftly as she sat, Debbie left. She had tried, she would tell her husband.

***

Tuesday rolled round and Debbie helped to arrange the seating. She suggested the group should maybe divide into two groups, but Peg, who ran the group, said no. It was good to have the beginners mix with the advanced; that way they could all help each other. There were only 12 in total, Peg added, so it wasn't that difficult to manage.

Debbie said nothing and sat in her usual spot – the third chair from the left, facing the door. She could see everyone who arrived, be near the top of the table where Peg sat, and hear all that was said. Her crochet work out before her, she started to stitch. The door opened in a rush, and in a flurry Rima toppled in.

"Sorry, sorry to be late. Bus very slow." Her breath came out in great bursts.

"Here, Rima, sit here, there's a chair next to me," Debbie called out. "There's no set time in this group, so you can never be late," she explained, as her new friend rooted around in her plastic carrier bag for her yarn and needle.

"Thank you."

"How are you today?" Debbie tugged some yellow yarn from its ball, working her stitches like the pro she was.

"Fine. You?"

"Me? Didn't sleep great last night, to be truthful. Leg cramps, you know."

"Oh. Your leg good now?"

"It's age, comes to us all. What are you working on?" Debbie touched the soft yarn Rima placed on the table.

"Baby blanket." Rima lifted the lilac yarn and held up her work.

"That's gorgeous. Your baby?" Debbie patted her own stomach then pointed at Rima.

"No. No. Friend."

The morning passed in a pleasant atmosphere. Chatting accompanied the women's business with their yarns and hooks. Debbie corrected Rima at times with her words, and the young woman proved to be polite company. Peg dismissed the women at noon and thanked them for coming. "See you next week."

***

The picture of the little child washed up on the beach was on everyone's mind. The sadness of it all. Each newspaper and television channel had it as their headline.

The group this morning was sombre. No tittle-tattle. Silence once more while they worked.

"Debbie, why is everyone sad?" Rima leaned towards her friend.

"The dead child in the sea, from the news. So awful." The older woman clutched her chest and shook her head. She then fiddled with the yarn on the table, having to rip back her work, the trellis stitch besting her.

"Yes, it sad. But she is one of many. I live with it." Rima turned away and started her crocheting.

Startled by Rima's words, Debbie paused. *What was going on in Callyhill? Under her own nose? It was in other countries, on the news. Surely it couldn't be in Debbie's home town?* She was nauseated by the girl's apparent acceptance of this unknown child's death, and struggled to understand.

"Want to go for a cup of tea?" Debbie couldn't shake the horrible feeling that now seeped through her. The photo of the child was difficult, but to think a person she knew understood it? No, it couldn't be. She must have misheard Rima. After all, her English wasn't great.

"Yes, the bakery?" Rima smiled.

***

They found a corner and sat with their drinks. Now and then, snippets of talk were heard around them, from the weather to the tragedies that were becoming everyday news. Pulling herself in closer, Debbie leaned in and spoke in a low voice.

"Rima, I have to ask. When we were speaking about the little girl, God rest her," Debbie made a quick sign of the cross on her chest and continued, "What did you mean by 'I live it'?"

"Debbie, it is long time ago, but I live it in my head day and night. Things I've seen never leave my memory. People losing their lives on journeys here and to other countries."

"Okay. I was curious, that's all. But of course, I understand." She picked at the fruit scone on the plate, her appetite not what it usually was. "No, Rima, sorry now, actually I don't understand. I don't understand at all." She pulled at her earring and twisted it. Her fingers were trembling as they pulled at the jewellery.

"Debbie, you kind and honest. All I say is I came to here like that little girl. In a boat. The boat I was on, many people. Young and old. A young girl died in sea; she fell when there was storm. Her name was Amira. A young boy, too, I no know his name. The girl, we shared water and biscuits. Her father was in boat, too. He cried for his daughter all time, and before we were found by big ship, he kept staring at the sea, not moving or talking."

Debbie flinched, her breath catching in her throat. She heard the rush of blood in her ears, speechless now. "Rima, this is terrible. What a horrible thing to have happen. How can you get over something like that?"

Rima shrugged. "You don't. You keep it here and push it back." The young woman first pointed to her head and then made pushing gestures with her hands.

Debbie nodded. She wasn't sure if she understood or not. She had a cosy home, a good husband, and here she was listening to a friend tell her about sea deaths, people searching for what she, Debbie, had enjoyed all her life. Nevertheless, she pressed ahead.

"Can I ask you some more questions? Would that be okay?"

"Yes. If I know words, I will answer." Rima folded her arms and rested them on the square glass-topped table, its wrought iron legs in a crisscross beneath it. The café was small but tastefully decorated with simple canvases on the wall, each with a slogan referencing coffee or tea. It was a café where friendly people served good fare.

"How did *you* get here? I know you said by boat, but to Ireland? From where, Syria? That must have been a long journey." The older woman's admiration for Rima increased with each passing moment. This young girl's strength was amazing.

"Aleppo. I started on a boat, yes. I arrive here in Ireland, four years ago, in a truck with others. I live in not this town, another one – Do-nah-big. I get bus here."

"I see, have you lived in Donaghbeg since you arrived in Ireland?"

"No. I live where I am told to live. I am in the centre, so I get moved around sometimes. It is not always good, but for me, I have no children, just me." Rima stared at Debbie, her deep brown eyes searching the other woman's face. If Rima was expecting Debbie to be judgemental, she was wrong.

"You've dealt with so much, and you're so young. Are all your family, your mum and dad, in Syria?" Debbie reached across and held her friend's hand. The young woman smiled and grasped the hand in hers.

"Yes. They want me to live a happy life. They pay to get me away. I was at college. I want to work and send them money, but I can't do this. I'm not accepted here yet." Rima sat upright as she spoke.

Debbie drank some tea. She held the cup in her free hand, not placing it down. She tried to understand how you would pack up a small bag and leave your family. Get on a boat to a place, any place, not knowing what waited for you. *Scared, that's what she'd be.* Frightened as hell, yet people were doing this all the time. People who were living in *her* country, fleeing war and persecution.

She trembled. Her hand felt clammy as she put down the cup. She withdrew her hand from Rima's grip and rubbed the temples of her forehead with her fingers, massaging them gently. A headache was rumbling, ready to hit with force. Rima's words had stressed her. A nice young woman like this one seated with her, forced to leave those she loved. *Wrong; it was all wrong.*

"Debbie, are you okay?"

"Rima, I don't like what you've said, it's upsetting." Her tummy growled with nausea, she wanted to lie down.

"But I tell truth!" Rima pushed back her chair.

"Oh yes, yes, of course, I believe you. Oh Rima, I didn't mean it that you upset me. I mean your story, the story of so many, I'm sure. I-I never really thought about it before. It's mind-numbing at the least, something you hear on the news, read in the papers. Not have it walking along your local main street. You… you make it real. How brave you are, Rima."

They sat, neither saying anything else. A sadness shared by the two women, floating like a dark cloud.

"I need to get bus. I must get back to centre!" Rima stood and picked up her bag.

Debbie got up and gave the woman a hug. "See you next Tuesday."

The centre. Debbie realised this was the Direct Provision Centre that Callyhill had rejected – not because they were horrible places for those living in them, but because of fear of those who were housed there.

***

The crochet group decided to mark International Women's Day by making a blanket. The ladies decided they would crochet a square in the colours of the country everyone was from – creating a blanket of flags. Although there were only 12 of them, they had eight nationalities to cater for, which surprised them all. Some of the women had lived for years in Ireland, coming initially to study then ended up working here, some marrying Irish partners. Others had not lived here so long, but they were all connected through their love of yarn.

Debbie searched on the computer for the various colours of each flag. She printed out the pictures of each one, then set about looking through her stash of yarn to see what she had. The following Tuesday she arrived armed with pictures and wool to share with the group. She liked to help Peg out.

Everyone was full of chatter and thrilled to be working on a group project. The librarian had said that when the blanket was finished, they would place it on a wall with a nice name plaque and group photo.

As the ladies worked their hooks, the colours of Brazil, Croatia, England, Germany, Poland, Syria, Italy, and Ireland began to take shape in squares.

"Rima, you're almost finished yours. Well done." Debbie praised the work of her friend.

"Thank you. I will stick on green stars with felt. That right word, felt? My crochet not so good to make them," she laughed. Everyone appeared in good spirits, the joint project bringing them closer.

"Why don't we have an international dinner night? We could all bring some dish from our countries for others to try. Anyone interested?" Peg suggested during their tea break. The flags had encouraged talk about their native homes, and her suggestion was met with agreement and a buzz of excitement.

The following Tuesday, Peg had more news for the group. The library staff were happy to host their dinner night and unveil their flag blanket, with the public invited to attend.

"We will have to dress up for this." Debbie's excitement spilled over to the others, all discussing their various wardrobes. Then she noticed that Rima was quiet, saying little.

"Are you okay?" She put a hand on the young woman's arm.

"I will ask for permission to be here from the centre. We have curfews. There's talk we will be moving. The owner is tired of trouble from some people who don't like us."

"What? Can he do that? Close you down?"

"Where there's direct provision centre, always protests."

Debbie remembered too well the protests against a centre being opened in Callyhill, and the shame sent a flush covering her neck and face. Councillor Sheila Nugent had swayed the town to refuse the centre for the wrong reasons, but Debbie had remained silent back then, leaving it to others in the town to deal with. Her husband had been horrified by her indifference – who really cared?

He had told her, "Don't condemn until you know the person and their story." He had been right all along.

"Try not to worry, Rima. It may not happen." Debbie didn't feel convinced, even as she spoke the words.

***

The local newspaper photographer was in attendance, as was Councillor Nugent. The room looked wonderful, with the tables set to one side, the array of food with little paper flags attached onto wooden skewers stuck into each dish, revealing where it was from. Plates upon plates of finger food were set out for self-service.

Then over on the wall, with a soft yellow cloth covering it, hung the blanket, fastened to two wooden slats for structure. The women were very proud of their work, and since Peg was the group leader, it was she who would unveil it after a short speech by the Councillor.

Debbie mingled with the others; her husband was there, too. Councillor Nugent spoke of the importance of women encouraging each other, being there for each other, like this wonderful crochet group was. She highlighted how people's nationalities did not make them different, but stronger. On and on she went until the librarian mentioned they could only stay in the building for an hour and a half. Everyone laughed at this, then Peg pulled the yellow cloth off and unveiled the colourful blanket.

Applause followed and cheering. Next up was the group photo. Debbie had spent the evening chatting and mixing with the locals who had come along, but now it was time for the group to be acknowledged. She couldn't see Rima, and asked Peg if she had she seen her.

The group leader admitted she hadn't; neither had the others.

Debbie searched outside, but the group needed her for the photo, so she returned inside. She couldn't smile. Her heart told her it was not good that Rima was absent.

With the social evening over, she stood and stared at the Syrian flag. Her husband put an arm around her and said it was time to go home. Walking out, she saw Councillor Nugent chatting to some people. Debbie walked over and excused herself for interrupting them.

"Sheila, can I ask you, is there any news about the Direct Provision Centre in Donaghbeg? I heard it might be closing." Debbie held her breath for the answer.

"Hello, Debbie. Yes, it closed last Thursday; there were some problems there. Well done on tonight, a great achievement for all involved."

"Except for our friend, Rima. That centre is her home," Debbie replied flatly. "Have a look at the blanket again, Sheila. It was people who crocheted each of those flags. They're all people, not problems."

Debbie turned and joined her husband. She couldn't stop the tears. Shame for not speaking up before mingled with sadness of Rima's absence.

Her husband put his arm around her. "Debbie, you did your best."

Once home, Debbie went straight to bed, doubting she would sleep. Her thoughts were on the red, white, and black flag, the perfect stitches, and the two green felt stars so carefully glued on by Rima.

A New Homeland

He watched the people surrounding him arguing with each other. They pushed and fought until one of them grew weary, and then it would stop. Clothes hung on any surface available, marking out each person's spot in this overcrowded camp. *Why did he leave? He was the head of his family, was he not? Where are they? Why did you leave them behind? Are they going to follow you?* Question after question that he gave no answers to. Everyone trying to be better than the next person. *Look at me, I have my family here, they are safe. Look at me, I have a job waiting, my cousin arranged it. Look at me, I will work and make my fortune.*

He curled up beneath the rough blankets he'd found abandoned. He had nothing of his own. Everything he possessed, he wore.

Raman pulled the covers over his head and blocked out the day. He did not deserve to be here. To be alive. The boat that rescued him and the others from the damaged raft had brought them ashore to stand on new soil. A new homeland. Some days, those who walked by him saw his tears and hugged him, whispering that he was safe now. *Life will begin.* His tears were not the happy ones of a man who had survived crossing the Mediterranean, but tears of guilt; a broken man whose family were dead. He could not save them, it was his fault, and he had failed in his duty as both husband and father.

A kick woke him up, and he peeped out from beneath the blankets.

"Want something to eat?"

Raman sat upright. "Why are you offering me this?"

"I have been watching you. You are not eating, just sitting and staring into the heavens. It is not a good way to be. Here, eat."

Raman took the bread and cheese and thanked the man. He chewed with delight, not realising how hungry he was.

"My name is Omar. I am here now many weeks. Where did you come from?" The man settled down beside Raman, took a water bottle from beneath his shirt, and offered him a drink.

"Thank you. I am Raman. I don't know how long I'm here."

"This place is not forever, but it is better to be here in the camp than out in the rolling sea. I will take my chances here than out there, yes?" The man laughed and drank from the bottle.

Sadness lurked within Raman, and he put down the food. "Thank you. I had enough."

"What is it that you torture yourself with?" Omar placed the remaining bread and cheese on some cloth and wrapped it, then he put it into a satchel that he wore across his body.

"I have lost everything. My family are gone, and it is my fault. I am not worthy of calling myself a husband or father." Raman's eyes welled up, and tears that he thought were not in him, fell.

"Raman, you are being hard on yourself. Tragedy is everyone's story here. Have we all not failed in some way? Your story is sad, but you are not alone. Tell me about your family."

Omar offered him a cigarette, but Raman shook his head. He did not like the habit, and in better days of the past, he would tell his daughters that only fools spent their money on cigarettes. He waited for his new friend to light the skinny rolled-up reefer and watched him inhale. A tiny weak waft of smoke lingered between them.

"I left because I had nothing. My wife and baby daughter were killed when our house was hit by a bomb as we were having our evening meal. Fatima was one year old, and my dear wife four years younger than me. My other daughter, Amira, was spared, as I was. With the house destroyed, what was the use of rebuilding it? The war was not going away. It would be foolish to think that it would not happen again. Of course, it was announced as an accident. The terrorists did not mean to target a residential area."

"Yes, your story is a common one. But where is Amira now? Is she with you, or back in your homeland with relations?"

"Amira is dead. Nine years old. The sea took her. It is angry with all of us sailing across it, I think, and it rears up and wipes out our rafts and boats with its temper." Raman's voice was strong, and he punched his fist into the ground.

"Losing your wife and children is sad, I am sorry for you. But you are here, and you must make your plans for your future. Do not let it be for nothing that you survived." Omar stubbed out the dying cigarette in the hard clay. Then he spat to the side and cleared his throat. "I do not have family. No woman wanted me." He laughed at his own words.

"Maybe here your luck will be brighter, and fortune will be yours," Raman offered.

"Maybe. But for now, I am planning on leaving and taking my chances with the others."

"How do you mean?" Raman leaned closer to Omar. He got the sense that Omar knew of something that others did not.

"See," Oman pointed to the wire fence over from them, "there is a way out of this camp. Some have left during the night, and they are met by people who bring them to a new life. It costs, of course, but you do not need to pay now. You can do that later. Come with me."

That night, Raman thought about Omar's words. *A new life. Wasn't that what he'd wanted for himself and Amira?* This camp was as suffocating as his old life, waiting to see what was next. In Syria, it was waiting for the next bomb, the next raid, whether there would be food for his family. Here it was no different, except that in place of bombs and raids, it was people. People who decided your fate, if you remained or were sent back. Waiting was waiting, regardless of what it is you were waiting for.

He slept little, disturbed by the crying of others for their old life and the fear of the new. When they had no more tears to spill, it was taken up with the weeping of newcomers.

By morning, Raman had made his decision. He met with Omar, and the two men shook hands. They would leave together. Walking along by the wired fence, they saw where it was weak; someone had covered the small opening with leaves and rubbish. The scratching of earth and the flattened grass on the outside marked the spot where people had escaped.

***

"Come quickly, here, here, into the van. Now." Orders were barked at Raman and Omar. Getting through the fence had gone without trouble. Now they were bundled into a van and being taken somewhere they did not know. After some time, others joined them in the cramped van. Bellies rumbled with hunger;

fear and sweat mingled in the claustrophobic air inside the vehicle. There were no windows, so they did not know if they remained in the countryside or were in a town.

An abrupt halt threw them sideways, and the doors were flung open. They were led to an old warehouse and some water was placed on a long table.

"Gather around," a man roared out to the hungry, tired group.

Men and some women did as they were told, but Raman and his friend hung back. They listened as they were informed what was going to happen. They would either stay here or be travelling on further, but they did not get to choose. The driver and his friends now owned them. Their debt was to be worked off – a payment for being smuggled in without being caught.

Raman and Omar looked at each other, fear swimming in their faces. Some of the refugees spoke out and said they did not agree to any payment. But they were immediately silenced. A slap, or a thump, or a threat, meant the matter was not for discussion.

When the women were taken out separately to another waiting van, their husbands and brothers cried after them, knowing the life ahead for them would be as prostitutes. Inside the warehouse, the men were divided into two groups. One would remain there and be put to work, scattered around the rural towns; the second group would go further south, where they would join those who had been trafficked before them. It was easier for those in the south to mingle in the large cities without drawing attention for their owners.

"You will work where you are told. When your debt is paid in full, you will receive papers allowing you to stay here. So, it is not so bad, eh? You will be fed and looked after. Just do your job and behave. That's all," the driver told the group that Raman and Omar were placed in. "Now, out. The truck is waiting."

It was cold, and their breath wafted into the late night. Raman blew into his hands while he waited for the instructions to board the truck.

"Where are we?" Omar asked a man nearby.

"England, I think. We are being sent towards London." The man shifted from foot to foot. He kept his head down not wanting to be seen talking.

"I think we are going to a ferry for Ireland. The truck driver is Irish; I heard another call out to him. This is his last trip, he said, and he is going home to Ireland," another man whispered.

Once Raman and the group were herded into the container of the truck, two more vans were heard pulling up outside, and shortly the container was full. People jostled against each other to try and claim space, but there was no point. More and more men were packed in, then the doors closed, and darkness blanketed them.

The heat from those crammed together mixed with their fear and sweat, the air hung heavily between them, and breathing became difficult. But the journey continued, with twists and turns, no stopping, and without food or water for those inside the container. Hours passed and Raman felt weak. People were falling, fainting on top of each other, others cried out for help, their attempts at banging on the walls too weak to draw attention.

How had he allowed this to happen? Raman asked himself. *Was he not an intelligent man?* His wife would be shocked if she knew where his plan for a new life had led.

Raman spoke quietly to himself, praying for forgiveness from his loved ones, begging their pardon for his failings to them. His eyes grew heavy, his breathing laboured. It didn't matter anymore if he lived or not.

The moaning from those around him became less as their lives surrendered to the hostility and wickedness that had captured them. Raman huddled closer to a side of the container. The jolts of the truck travelling were the only feeling of life as time became irrelevant.

Shouting roused him from his stupor. Blaring sirens drowned the voices outside, and then the container doors were flung open. Raman covered his eyes, the daylight blinding him, the rush of fresh cold air striking him awake. He heard orders being given, men in uniforms jumping into where he and the others lay.

"Quick, get the paramedics. We need medical attention urgently."

Time passed in a blur. Body after body of those who had given up were taken away. Lights flashed – blue, red, white – more shouting, people in uniforms rushing here and there, and Raman wondered what was next. Did he want to know? It would be better surrendering to the fading strength of his body, to not fight. His sweet wife and daughters were waiting for him; he should go join them, be with them.

He felt his body being lifted, and someone was saying, "Stay with me, man, stay with me."

Raman slowly opened his eyes. The truck driver stood nearby, in handcuffs, his head down, eyes on the ground.

"Your name?" a uniformed man was asking the driver.

"Brian," the handcuffed man replied, not raising his head to look at the scene around him.

Raman closed his eyes again. His breathing hurt. The voices of those who carried him faded.

He saw Amira first – running, smiling. "Baba, Baba, look it's me."

The heavy guilt Raman carried had vanished. He felt young once more and opened his arms out to his daughter. Beyond her stood his sweet wife and little Fatima.

He was home. Together once more.

A Tough Workday

Joe sat on the empty beer keg in the laneway out the back of the pub. Around him the blare of horns, sirens, and shouts from the busy streets. It was hot; steam from nearby restaurant kitchens burst out of vents, carrying the aromas of so many countries with them – Indian, Mexican, Lebanese, and more. A whole world existed here on this patch alone. *How many years had he been here now? Was it 12, 14?* Each time he stepped from his apartment to the streets, he was in awe of this city – its punch of life hit him every day; at night, the neon-drenched streets and shopping malls.

It was his break. Fifteen minutes to catch a breath before launching back into cocktails and beers for his many customers. He remembered the scandalous gasp from his mother Sheila one time she'd phoned him, back in the early days, and he'd told her he was busy with a Sex on the Beach. Cocktails had yet to reach Callyhill back then.

Joe took a breath, a deep one, and saw his reflection in a nearby window and ignored it. Being hot, many of the businesses had their rear doors open. He knew the voices he heard arguing, laughing, and calling to others. Litter gathered around the bins where trash overflowed.

His mother.

If asked to describe her, he'd say a difficult woman. She had her good points, it was just that she rarely showed them. Joe and his brother had both left Callyhill as soon as they could manage it. They were close; closer than most brothers would be. Charlie was three years older than Joe, but even now that they were thousands of miles apart, they were in regular contact.

He had always known this day would come, but he'd never thought about what it would mean when it did happen. Now Joe was in a dilemma. Charlie's text remained unanswered. And that was because he did not know what to reply.

"Hey, Joe, you alright, man?" It was Randy. They managed the bar together.

"Randy, what are you doing here? Your shift is not for another three hours."

"Mate, Gina called me. She told me your news. Listen, you need to go. Just go."

"Thanks, but I'm okay. I can finish the shift." Joe didn't want to go to his apartment. He didn't want this day to be different to any other. He was a man of routine. He wasn't the sentimental one of the Nugents. Nope, that was Charlie.

"Whatever. I'll stick around in case you change your mind. No rush back from this break, okay?"

Joe nodded and caught his reflection on the window again. This time, he saw a man he did not recognise. He hadn't noticed the change, the lines catching around his eyes, fine marks that crinkled up more when he smiled. His hairline was receding a bit, too. Plus, the stubble that he took as being sexy was anything but. *How had this happened? When did he go from being 19 to almost 34?*

He pulled out his phone. He needed to reply to Charlie, who would be waiting on an answer to his message. The time difference was what: five, six hours? So, Charlie was late afternoon now. He punched in his pin to unlock the mobile, then brought up Charlie's text.

Charlie: Will u be coming home?

What to say? Joe scratched his head. A slight dampness covered his brow, reminding him of when he and Charlie would run through the farmer's fields playing space wars. The different corners had been their universes, the cattle the aliens who inhabited them. Scaling trees were their rockets, and the farmer shouting at them to get off his land was the nasty villain they had come to fight. They'd return home dripping of sweat from running around. Simple fun.

He wondered if those fields were still there. Maybe a housing estate or a shopping centre claimed their playing patch now. Joe's memory of Callyhill was fading. His life here in New York was not just far away in miles, but in every way possible.

His mother had refused to visit when her youngest son decided he was going to stay here. She'd warned him against it. Told him no good would come of him being illegal in another country. He was only working in a bar, not running a giant company, she'd scolded. He could do that at home in Ireland.

When he first arrived in the Big Apple on a holiday visa, Joe had soaked up the culture and the way of life. There was always a buzz, even on his down-days when homesickness took over; always a place to go, something to see or do. It was the choice, that's what had lured him in. He could go anywhere and be anyone. There were no limits put on him and his dreams.

"Don't be foolish, Joe. You need to come back and go to college. Then you can go back to the States and get a proper job if you want, though I don't see why you would. If you want, I'll see about getting you a job down in Murray's bar here at the weekends."

"Jesus, Mam, I don't want college. I'm happy here."

"I'll get Charlie to talk to you."

"What on earth are you on about?"

"You know what I mean. Charlie is away, too. I thought one of you would stay here with me, be near me like."

"Mam, London is only across the water, and here just a bit further."

"I want you home, Joe."

"What about my brother? Why can't he go home?"

"Is it too much to ask after all I did on my own, after your father died? What if you both have children?"

"Mam, you're over-reacting. I don't know about Charlie, but I've no plans to settle. I'm staying for a while, and I'll be back when I'll be back. Going to go now, Mam. Mind yourself."

He could hear her now, the sharpness of her voice, the tone hinting at how wronged she felt, the pity-me whinge thrown in after the long pauses. Joe hated it. Hated the phone calls home. Never did she ask how he was, only when was he coming back.

When he video-called, she refused to answer, saying it would break her heart to see him and know she couldn't hug him. Joe had almost laughed at that. *Hug him?* His mother had never hugged them. Men didn't need to be hugged; they were men, not sissies, she'd inform them.

The sun was beating down upon him now. New York in August was a sauna; waves of heat shimmered giving everything you saw a mirage effect. People passing by each other, phones out, water bottles, pastries eaten on the go, rushing, life here was lived in a fast gear.

Unlike Callyhill.

He recalled a sleepy town with one large supermarket, two corner shops, poor internet, more pubs than any other business, and one set of traffic lights. Unless you were into the GAA – the holy grail of sport, and a rite of passage for so many – there was nothing for you to do at the weekends. Buses to the city were rare and unreliable, plus no way did his mother allow him or Charlie to travel to the city without her. It wasn't that she was protective, wrapping them in cotton wool. No, it was that she needed to be in control. What did they want to go there for? How much were they thinking of spending?

When he first said this to Charlie over a few sneaked cans in the field amongst the bales of hay one summer evening, his brother had nodded in agreement.

"She's that for sure. I think she's harder on you, being the baby," Charlie said.

Once the cool beers worked their way into their minds, it all came spilling out, the honesty of their thoughts. Their mam was a control freak. No birthday parties for them; she wanted her house to be tidy. Two days in the year, that's all, but their mother refused. No school tours; she didn't know enough about where they were going. No mobile phones, no PlayStation, no internet, no sweets between Monday and Friday, no, no, no… It went on and on. But Charlie and Joe had each other. That's what got them through after their dad died.

When Charlie went to London through work, he told her he would be there for six months. Then the phone calls started. She kept asking when he'd be back to Ireland. It was her interference that nailed it for Charlie; a phone call too many. When their mother rang his company's Irish office and demanded her son be brought back from England, Charlie left the company – both from embarrassment and anger – and found work in a new firm in London. He phoned to tell her he was staying there permanently and refused to share where he worked or lived.

Joe recalled his mother's silence in the house after that episode. He wasn't to mention his brother's name. How dare Charlie not come home? She knew enough people to ask for a job for him in Callyhill.

Ted, her friend from the town's committee on which their mother was a very active member, told her she shouldn't stop the boys living their life their way. It was Ted, too, who encouraged Joe to apply for a holiday visa to the States.

"Let them travel, Sheila. If you don't, you'll regret it."

Ted, their mother's loyal friend. *Had he seen their mother's overbearing ways and helped the boys escape? Where was Ted now?* Joe would have to ask Charlie. What a shame he had let that connection go. That man had been their saviour so many times growing up. He would wink at them when he would be trying to win their mother over to whatever it was they wanted. A kind man; never a bad word from him. He even put up with their mother's rules and expectations and rarely argued with her.

He and Charlie often suspected that Ted was in love with their mother, but by not marrying her, he got to go home and take a break from her demanding ways.

An argument nearby shook Joe from his trips down nostalgia lane, and he stirred. His head filled with all the memories as he stood up, stiff from sitting on the keg, he stretched his body and wiped his face with his bar apron. He placed his phone back into his jeans pocket. He would text Charlie later.

The darkness of the bar dazed him for a few seconds, the music filling him up and pushing all thoughts of Callyhill from his mind. He grabbed some empty glasses as he passed by the tables and slipped behind the bar counter – a long, walnut timbered top, high stools along one side, dishes of salty peanuts and chips dotted about on it. Chips. It had taken him forever to change his way of thinking when he first arrived here. Chips here were crisps back home, and fries here were chips back home.

Gosh, a bag of Tayto cheese and onion crisps would be good right now. The happy face of Mr. Tayto smiling on each packet. *Did some punter say that the Tayto man had a theme park now in Ireland?* He looked around. There was never a lull in customers. The regulars sipped their pints, and the tourists giggled and snapped selfies with the large bronze statue of the Irish wolfhound that looked down on all who came through the doors.

"Well, are you going home?" Randy walked up to him, his face serious. His mouth was a tight, thin line, while a slight frown crowned his face. He had to know.

"I dunno. What would you do?"

"I told you many times to go legal here, mate. Now, well, it's gonna be difficult."

"Yeah, I know. Time just flew past. No day was the right day, you know, to set things in motion."

Joe knew he had never gone the legal route because he had been afraid of losing. If he lost, then he would be deported, never to return. He was scared. New York was his life. He was free here. Charlie had visited over the years; it hadn't stopped them from being brothers. It was only Mam who refused to come. Phone calls stopped, drizzling down to her birthday and Christmas.

"Look, you need to tell Charlie today. Don't they bury them fast in Ireland?" Randy walked away, greeting a customer and taking her order.

"Shit, shit, shit." Joe pounded the counter with his fist. A few looked his way then returned their eyes to the television screens they had been watching.

By seven that evening, Joe had finished his shift and was sitting in a café not far from his apartment block. Today had been a tough one. He pulled his phone from his jacket pocket, the coffee sitting before him going cold, untouched.

Joe: What r u doing? U going home?

The town would talk about him. Callyhill would dine out on the news once it was known. Sheila Nugent's son, selfish, no respect, dreadful for the poor woman. He could see it, hear it, the whispering, the nudges in the shop queues. Did they hear the latest about the Nugent boy? Boy! That made him laugh out loud. He was a man, but at home he would still be seen as the Nugent boy.

His phone beeped, a reply.

Charlie: Suppose so. Easier for me, though.

Joe: I'm a mess. Don't know what to do. I want to, but then I don't.

Charlie: She didn't make it easy. Will u go bk to NY if u come to Callyhill?

Strange how Charlie called it Callyhill and not home, Joe realised. *How did he do that? Was he not the one who always brought up their childhood games? When had he cut himself off from his place of birth? Had he erased it from his thoughts?*

Joe: Need to know how u can do that. Call it Callyhill, not home.

Charlie: What? It's Callyhill, that's it. I live here, London. This is home.

Joe: But our childhood, the past, u know, stuff we did, school, friends.

Charlie: What about it? It happened, it's over, life's here. U ok?

Joe: Yeah, yeah, fine. Thinking too much, I guess. Can I ask u something, want an honest answer, ok?

Charlie: Ok, shoot.

Joe: If u were me, would u travel bk for it?

Charlie: Tough one. Part of me says I should out of duty. Yet, shouldn't we be rushing there if we loved her? Would we be hesitating? Even if it stopped u from returning to the US?

Joe: Christ, Charlie, now I feel fucking awful. I did love her, she was our mam, after all. Not the greatest one, but she was ours.

Charlie: You asked me to be honest.

Joe: I did. Thought u were the sentimental one in the family ☺

Charlie: Grew up, didn't I? So?

Joe: I'll think about it and get back to u tomorrow. Who's handling the arrangements?

Charlie: Good old Ted.

Joe: I was thinking of him earlier. I'd nearly go home for his sake.

The night stretched out. Each time Joe dozed, his mother's face was before him. He tried to recall the happy shared family moments, but failed. He sat up in bed and Googled Tayto Park Ireland. Then he went to Google maps and found Callyhill. How much it had changed and grown. Street names he didn't recognise. Shopping centres. The school had expanded, plus the library was new and modern. A bustling town, it appeared. Their fields were untouched, just altered a bit – now a town park equipped with a playground and sports pitches.

This was a different Callyhill. He Googled some more.

Christ, how did he not know this? Did Charlie? Mam had been the Councillor of Callyhill! But she hated everything and everyone; there were others like her who actually voted for her!

He read on, article after article of her three years in office. Shops opened; protests attended. Photos of her smiling for the cameras. But her eyes held no warmth. Sheila played the part. He found photos, too, of Ted – him and Sheila at the town committee functions.

Joe rushed to the bathroom but couldn't throw up. His stomach churned with anger. Seeing another side to his mother's life, one she never thought to tell them about, sickened him. He had asked numerous times. He would say, 'What did you do today, Mam? Are you going out?' And always the same answer: 'No, nothing to share, life is life.' And that great pause of woe-is-me, all alone.

Did it matter if Charlie knew this side of their mother? If he did, it hadn't been mentioned, so he believed his brother was in the dark, too. Joe looked in the mirror, his reflection once again forcing him to see what was under his nose. His mother's lack of interest, lack of courtesy towards her sons. *Why had she kept it quiet? Were both her boys such disappointments to her? Did she consider them at all when she went about Callyhill? Ever speak about them to others?* He would never know.

Joe returned to his bed and sat and listened to the sounds of New York. Pulling out his phone, he brought up Charlie's messages. Reading the earlier texts they'd shared, his thumb swiped over them, deleting each one. Turning into the wall, he messaged Charlie and dropped his phone to the ground.

Joe: Say hello to Ted for me.

Michal

He watched the teenagers gathered at the gateway of a boarded-up house to the right on their road. Six, maybe seven of them standing around, nothing to do. One, on a bicycle, did his wheelies and flicks of the back wheel in the air while riding it, but the others weren't even watching, especially the two girls who leant against the wall. It was all for their benefit, this daredevil stuff, Michal reckoned. But the young girls kept their heads down, eyes on their phones instead.

Michal had also jumped through hoops to keep his Alicja. He had believed her tears, her pleading for forgiveness. Wrapping his arms around her, he had held her close and told her it was okay, it was all okay, and that her affair in their native Poland was well behind them. Michal knew he had played his part in her indiscretion. He had become lazy, lounging in front of the television, refusing her offers to go out with her. Moving here had been their new start – a new country, a chance for them to leave their problems behind.

Arriving in Ireland had brought new hope. Michal finding work on the farm meant it was easier to source a place to rent, and Alicja had picked up work, too, some shifts cleaning in a small supermarket. They were happy again. It was different here. At first, they went for walks, they held hands, and they bought bikes and went on long cycles into the Irish countryside.

The closed-up house where the young kids hung around was an eyesore amid the others lining the street. Michal's was the last home on the cul-de-sac, tucked away in the corner, facing the gable-end of another home. It wasn't the prettiest of views. In fact, it was depressing looking out at the dirty, pimpled wall. No-one passed their house, only cars turning to go back down the road. But it was theirs, they were together, and that's what mattered to Michal.

"Lunch is ready," Alicja called out to her husband, and he joined her in the kitchen.

The days were long for her without friends. She was pale, and the unhappiness in her eyes spilled out over her pretty face, like a mask. He watched her now, eating in silence.

"Did you do some of your English homework this morning?" Michal spoke as he tucked into the salami sandwiches.

"I tried. But cannot understand. It is so hard. Why do I speak English at all?" she pouted, reminding him of the teenagers outside.

"Because it makes life easier if you understand what is being said to you." His tone was encouraging and filled with lightness.

"It's okay for you, Michal. You are smart, but I'm not. You shouldn't make me do stuff that's hard." She lifted her full coffee cup to her lips, her fingers tightened around the mug.

"I'm not making you, Alicja. I'm trying to make life here easier." This time, he spoke more softly. He looked downwards, holding a breath. It was clear where this conversation was going, draining him of energy before she continued.

"Easier? Why change who I am?"

"No-one is saying you must change. I don't want to argue, sweetheart. I'm only trying to help." He finished his meal and went outside again to the front gate.

The youths had moved on, leaving their rubbish behind them. He looked at his garden with its trimmed lawn, full flower pots sitting by the front door, the windows polished and the paintwork clean. The gate where he now stood had also had a makeover of fresh paint. Gone were the rusty patches and the unoiled latch. Michal had worked his DIY skills magic, and now it hung proudly – the entrance to his and Alicja's fresh start. *He'd made the effort. Couldn't she?*

He needed to do something to stop himself from overthinking, as her lack of interest niggled beneath his skin. He had an idea. Michal grabbed a plastic bag from under the stairs and went over to gather the cans and wrappers the teenagers had left behind. He walked around the abandoned house, picking up the litter. Once he had completed this good deed, he felt invigorated; a buzz ran through him. With a strong stride, he went home and pulled out his gardening tools.

"What you doing for?" Alicja leant against the front door frame and watched her husband clean up the front garden of the sad-looking house. "Wasting time. It will be same again in few days." Shaking her head, she returned inside. She didn't hear his reply; she hadn't waited for it.

The weeks passed, with Michal maintaining the garden of the unoccupied house. He painted the window sills and fixed the gate. One day, a neighbour he didn't know came out to join him. Jan washed the windows, and his wife brought them coffee and biscuits when they took a break. He was from Latvia, as was his wife; they'd lived here now over four years.

Michal and Jan chatted until late in the evening, sharing their thoughts on leaving their countries, life now, and football.

"Are you happy you came here?" Jan asked.

"Yes. It has a good reputation. I met Irish at Euro football championships. Their football fans are best, but I won't tell any Irishman." Both men laughed.

"Yes, I like it here, too, but they can be hard to understand at times. They say something, but it can mean something else. They say, *sure I will,* which means no, and *it was mad,* meaning it was great. I know we do the same, but to hear these local ways in different language is confusing." Jan shook his head to emphasise his point, and the two men laughed at the funny Irish ways.

"Alicja doesn't speak much English." Shrugging his shoulders, Michal finished the coffee he was drinking. Then he continued, "Is there a Latvian community here?"

"No. Only a handful of us. I believe you Polish have big numbers here, though, even in Callyhill."

"Yes, come along and meet some. We watch football together. It is only place here I think my wife is happy, being with other Polish."

***

Alicja stood at the sink, washing up the breakfast things. Michal crept up on her. "Happy anniversary, love." He slipped his arms around her waist, kissed her neck, and spun her around to face him.

She laughed. "You silly man, it's not our wedding anniversary. But I will happily accept whatever gift you've bought me." She snuggled into his chest, breathing in his scent.

"It's our one year arriving in Ireland anniversary," he whispered into her ear then squeezed her to him some more.

Her body against him went limp, the magic of their closeness gone. She pulled away from him and turned to start her chores again. Michal threw his hands in the air. He gave up. *What was he to do?* Words crept up his throat, but he pushed them down. The weariness of arguing didn't appeal.

After a while, Alicja gave up attending the language classes. When Michal asked her to join him over at Jan's for an invited evening, she said she didn't want to go. They were not her people.

"It's not about being Irish, Alicja, you know that. It's making friends. If we were back home, you would make effort to speak to people who were not Polish. You did in your old job."

"Oh, throw in my face, go ahead. You not forgiven me, have you? Bring it up again. You like to remind me of the restaurant and Ivan."

Raising his voice a little, his words were shadowed with bitterness as he spoke through clenched teeth, trying to restrain the urge to shout in reply. "What? Don't be stupid. I'm saying you worked in a restaurant and served tourists," he told her. "You made talk and understood them, didn't you? I didn't say it to upset you. Believe me, I've forgotten your close friend, Ivan." Cracking his knuckles, he then grabbed the bottle of vodka from the kitchen table and fled to Jan's.

***

Michal settled into life, with Jan coming around to watch football matches at the weekends. Alicja and Jan's wife were polite to each other, but Alicja made no real effort. She met with the other Polish women and formed her friendships there. But Michal knew he was losing her. Nothing he did was enough. She went to work and came home. No longer did she go for walks with him; the bicycles lying rusted by the side of the house. Meals became silent, Alicja on her phone, Michael making small talk to the kitchen cabinets.

***

"Surprise!"

Alicja lifted her head at Michal's words but remained seated on the sofa. She was tired of his cajoling and pretence of happiness. Her raised eyebrows asked what now?

"Don't you want to know what this is?" He flapped the envelope in his hand about in the air. His eyes were glowing with happiness, his breaths short with excitement.

"Tell me." Her tone was flat, disinterested. "Another anniversary?" she snapped, as she put her phone down on the cushion.

"A weekend to Poland... well, four days actually. But since you're not interested, I can cancel it." He turned and walked away.

Her hands were around his neck and her legs clamped her to his hips before he got to the door. "What? Really, Michal? Oh yesssss, oh, you're the best."

He held her on his back and laughed at her childish playfulness. She kissed his neck, his hair, pulled gently on his ear with her teeth. Old times; it felt like old times ran through his mind.

She packed and chatted nonstop the night before she left, her excitement lighting the house with life. Michal listened to her chatter: what she had bought for her parents, her sister, her Nan. What she would bring back to him, anything in particular?

"Just you," he told her. "Just you. He went to her and kissed her lips with longing. She pulled from him, but a smile told him she wanted him, too.

Their night was blissful, their lovemaking fervent and breathless. Alicja was alive; she no longer existed but lived. He could tell by the way she walked, she spoke, she loved. And this coming trip home had reawakened her.

"Such a pity you aren't coming, Michal, it would make it even more perfect." She held his hand as he saw her to catch the bus to the airport.

"I know, love, but there will be a next time, and we will visit for longer," he replied, forcing the cheerfulness in his voice, smiling with his mouth but not from the heart. This trip on her own proved for him he trusted her, he scolded himself.

He placed her bag beneath the bus, into the luggage hold. Then he pulled her in for a last embrace before she got on. "Don't forget to come back." He pulled on her nose and tickled her waist.

"See you on Tuesday, Michal. I love you." Then once seated, she waved out to him.

"I love you, too," he mouthed to his wife, as the bus pulled away from the stop.

***

Going about his work on the farm, he fretted each day she was away. The cattle felt his distress, and a few ran from him as he walked through the field. He called out to them. They were his girls, he joked with his boss, as together they prepared the animals for milking. Ned nodded in response with understanding.

How many times had he shared his secrets with them? Now he watched his farmhand do the same, sharing in a low voice whatever it was that burdened the young man this weekend.

MICHAL: Will be waiting for you. 7.30pm, yes? Xx Safe trip. Love you xx

ALICJA: Yes.

Michal stood at the bus stop. He watched the traffic coming over the hill on the south side of the town. The main street curved as it left Callyhill on the road to the airport. The traffic had quietened now, most already home from their day's work.

The pigeons kept him company as he waited, letting the crows do the work of pulling the waste from the bins outside the chipper. The crows had it all worked out, grabbing what was in their way of the food and discarding it on the path. Then, with a victorious cawing, the bird would pull out some ketchup-covered chips, part-eaten burger, or crusts from a sandwich, and fly off with his dinner. The smaller birds, the jackdaws and rooks, took the leftovers, with the pigeons cooing as they tried to muscle in on the meal, too.

Others waiting around him moved forward to the kerb; the bus was coming. Michal stood back. His palms were sweaty, and he felt his heart was going too fast. *How would she be? Had he done the right thing in sending her away?* He skimmed the tinted windows of the vehicle as it drew up alongside the footpath, but he couldn't see her.

"Michal!" her voice reached him, a high-pitched cry as she ran and jumped into his arms.

She was here.

"I missed you so much, Alicja. Welcome home, sweetheart."

Pulling her travel case, he held her hand and they strolled leisurely home, while Alicja chatted non-stop about her long weekend.

***

Michal saw the light in his wife's eyes when she spoke about their families, friends, and the things she had done in Poland. Each morning, she started the day with, "Did I tell you about…?" He heard the same stories over and over, but on every occasion he would shake his head and say, "I don't think so. Tell me now."

Months passed, and Alicja was still happy to stay in her own bubble. Work and home. She spent more time on her phone. Now and then, she would show Michal some of the silly messages, or they would serve as a reminder for her of another story about her Polish trip. Michal could not get over how much she had packed into her short stay. So he asked his boss for time off to travel with her next time.

Alicja screamed with delight when he announced the weekend away – this time together.

"The flights are cheap when you book in advance," he said to Jan, as they shared a beer one evening. The men had become firm friends.

Poland proved to be refreshing for both Michal and his wife – a real tonic. And Michal admitted he had missed it, as they sat on the plane back to Ireland. His words only fuelled Alicja in putting more pressure for them to return, but he explained they had a good life in Ireland, earning more, with their own home. They would need to keep saving some more before they should consider a move back for good, he told her. She pouted and sulked at his words.

He asked her to cycle with him on his weekends off, explore the castle ruins that were out beyond the meat factory. But she refused. Her bike gathered rust and cobwebs. Orange-brown marks streaked the paintwork where it leant against the house wall, its wheels gone flat, the chain seized up from the winter weather.

The brief trips home only served to fuel her argument to leave Ireland. Her skin glowed on her return, the energy pumping through her. But the peaks of happiness dissolved as the days went by on her return. She would withdraw a little and their cosy evenings lessened while she curled up on the armchair, head down, her fingers flicking over the phone keypad.

***

It came while he was at work.

Alicja was over in Poland, enjoying another weekend on her own. Michal was walking the boundary fields for openings that the winter storms had created. The cattle were not yet out from their sheds, so now was the time to secure any gaps in the ditches. Ned, the boss man was with him.

ALICJA: Michal, I can't do it. I stay in Poland. I'm sorry.

Nothing more. Not a phone call; not another message. He dropped the hammer in his hand and flung the phone into the thorny briars where he was working. Ned tapped him on the shoulder and led him back to the farmhouse, the work unfinished for now.

***

The house lost its appeal. It was now just a place to lay his head, to shelter from prying eyes and unwanted questions. The garden became invaded; the weeds speared their heads up, and dandelions peppered the pathway. Litter blew under the gate, travelling further in with every breeze. The flowerpots standing sentry at the doorway were now unwelcoming and overgrown. Some days the curtains remained drawn. To those on the street, the house looked lonely and unloved.

The teenagers gathered again at the house Michal had tended to, it too forgotten, the garden matching his own. Their laughter invaded Michal's misery.

Jan tried to help, but nothing eased Michal's pain. He had tried, hadn't he? Jan agreed he had. It was Alicja. But that did not console the broken man. Turning over in his bed with a hangover, he slept on, letting Ned down yet again.

Vodka became his confidante, and most evenings he told his fears to the full glass before him and bitched about his wife's heartlessness. The knocking on the door made him angry, as he roared at whoever it was to go away. He didn't want pity.

The television was turned up loud to drown out the voices he heard in his head. Whisperings who told him to leave the world outside, to stay away from its viciousness that stole happiness from people, revealing their flaws. He was a man who could not keep his wife, not in any country. No other woman would want him. Day by day, the mutterings drowned any motivation, suffocating any positive thought that surfaced, destroying his appetite for everything.

***

The summer's heat peeped through a split in the dirty curtains. Its rays stretched out, long and narrow, across the sitting room, piercing the dusty air. In the corner, the blaring television. The constant noise helped Michal keep at bay those whispers inside his mind: *a failure, useless, unworthy.*

He lost his job. Ned couldn't depend on him.

"Go back to Poland, lad, you've family and friends there,' the farmer told him kindly. "Don't be too proud to return. The drink ruined many an Irishman in England. She would have left you no matter where you were. Trust me."

Ned's strong hand on Michal's shoulder was fatherly, and the farmhand wept unashamed tears as he lurched down the passageway. The farmer's words rang in his ears: *Don't be too proud, lad.*

Once home, he sat and poured a vodka, filling the pint glass. He couldn't return to Poland; he could not bear to see Alicja with any other man. He would stay in his house and never go back outside again. The voices visited, stuffing his head, pouring from his ears, jumping from his mouth, arguing with the man on the telly who promised warm days, but it rained instead. They lied. Everyone lied. Alicja lied.

He listened to them more and more. *You don't need anyone. Stay inside, this is your place, can't disappoint anyone in here, let Alicja go, she didn't deserve you, Ned will get more help, you will be master of your own life. Always trying to please others, a fool's idea, nothing more...*

He wandered from room to room, shouting at the emptiness, calling out to Alicja, cursing her, too. What had Ivan got that *he* couldn't give her? The sleepless nights followed the torment-filled days. There were too many utterings inside his mind. They confused him, and he couldn't fight them on his own. Only the vodka silenced them.

The mornings came around too quickly. His head always hurt, and the voices would soon start. Downstairs, he stared at the mess he was living in. Shame crept through him; this was not the real Michal. Reaching for a beer, he heard laughing and the sound of a mower. He shook himself to clear away the sounds, but the laughter and chatting continued. *Had he lost his mind?* He went and peeped out from behind the lounge curtains.

Jan and others were clearing Michal's garden. The gate was painted, no litter papered his footpath. He went to the door and opened it with a shaking hand.

As his neighbours stopped and looked at Michal, Jan approached and put an arm around him. "You helped others, now we help you. It will not always be this bad. Let us help you to be happy again."

Tears welled up, and Michal shook with relief and hugged his friend.

"Now, go shower and shave, and we will work together, yes?" Jan urged.

Nodding, Michal retreated. Jan was right; happiness could be his again. He liked Ireland; he liked Callyhill. He would not be too proud to accept help. Ned was right, too; she would have left no matter where they lived.

Searching for some rubbish bags, Michal started to clear the empty boxes and cartons from the sitting room. But as he placed packed rubbish bag after rubbish bag by the kitchen door, it felt as though there was still something wrong. He heard the clamour of work from outside.

"That's it!" he shouted.

Racing around the house, he threw open all the curtains and windows. As light flooded in, Michal closed his eyes and took a deep breath. A long battle lay ahead, but he would rebuild his life, one day at a time, with the help of his friends.

The End

For The Reader

Definition of the terms refugee, asylum seeker and migrant are available at https://www.amnesty.org/en/what-we-do/refugees-asylum-seekers-and-migrants/#definitions

The terms "refugee", "asylum seeker" and "migrant" are used to describe people who are on the move, who have left their countries and have crossed borders. The terms "migrant" and "refugee" are often used interchangeably but it is important to distinguish between them as there is a legal difference.

Below is a short definition for these terms:

A refugee is a person who has fled their country of origin and is unable or unwilling to return because of a fear of being persecuted because of their race, religion, nationality, membership of a particular social group or political opinion.

An immigrant is one who moves into another country whereas an emigrant is a person who moves away from his own country.

An economic migrant is someone who leaves his or her country of origin purely for financial and/or economic reasons. Economic migrants choose to move in order to find a better life and they do not flee because of persecution. Therefore, they do not fall within the criteria for refugee status and are not entitled to receive international protection.

About This Collection

Inspiration for the collection came from various observations. Watching an advertisement on TV for donations to war-ridden Syria, a family's home was blown up. I wondered about the family: did anyone survive? If they did, what was next for them? This is how my story Go Be Happy came about. The story of Michal, and his wife Alicja, was written after noticing a sense of loneliness in some of the immigrants in cafés, sitting by themselves, their heads down, hoods up. In another story, The Birthday Party, the choice of ever moving to live elsewhere was eliminated by family events. Yet, in Dear Mom and Dad, family duty is the reason behind Katie leaving her home to help those she left behind.

So, there are many reasons for people who search for new beginnings – war and conflict being the biggest. But I concentrated on those affected by family, home life, religion, or society forcing their decision. I settled on a fictionalised town in rural Ireland. Which is why a few of the characters pop up in more than one story. The stories are all fictional, I hope to give readers something to consider about our ever-changing communities and the positives we stand to gain from each other.

Please Review

Dear reader,

Thank you for taking the time to read this book. I would really appreciate if you could spread the word about it and if you purchased it online, if you would leave a review.

Thank you

About the Author

Mary Bradford is the Irish published author of four novels and several novellas. Living now in her native county Cork, she previously lived in Dublin for 20 years. Mary enjoys crochet and crafting which gives her a chance to unwind from stories that may be tumbling around in her mind. Her short stories continue to appear in newspapers, magazines and anthologies. Mary still harbours the dream of owning a home by the sea, be it a tent or a small cottage to which she can escape and read. All her work is available online with Amazon and BuyTheBook.ie. Mary is now a Nana and loves every minute of this new chapter in her life.

Books published by Mary are included overleaf.

Other Books by the Author

A Bakers Dozen: Thirteen Short Stories To Enjoy With A Coffee

Life is full of twists and turns, and every story has a lesson to teach. Journey through tales that tug at the heartstrings and where the kindness of strangers shines brighter than the darkest moments. Whether you're seeking inspiration, solace, or just a good story, this book invites you to pick a tale, pour yourself a warm drink, and let these pages transport you

My Husband's Sin - The Lacey Taylor Story Book 1

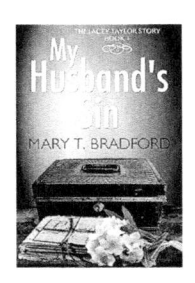

Lillian Taylor's bitter words—calling her youngest daughter, Lacey, *My Husband's Sin*—haunted the family for years. But what did they mean?

After Lillian's death, Lacey uncovers a devastating secret that shatters the fragile bonds holding the Taylor family together. As the truth unravels, it sends shockwaves through her siblings' lives, forcing them to confront their own struggles with love, resentment, and identity.

Lacey's journey to uncover the full story becomes a shared reckoning, where every answer raises new questions, and only one person holds the key to the family's salvation.

Don't Call Me Mum - The Lacey Taylor Story Book 2

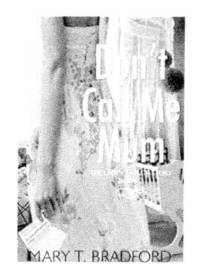

Lacey Taylor and Cora Maguire couldn't be more different. Lacey is young, kind-hearted, and longing for connection, while Cora, a celebrity dress designer, is fiercely ambitious and prioritizes business above all else.

When Lacey tracks down her birth mother, she hopes for a bond that will fill the missing pieces of her life. But Cora, driven by success, doesn't have room for sentimentality.

As events unfold, Lacey is forced to confront what family truly means. With heartbreak, manipulation, love, and loss, this gripping novel will leave you wondering who will pay the ultimate price.

No More Secrets- The Lacey Taylor Story Book 3

Harriet is stunned by the unexpected gift she receives on her eighteenth birthday—a trust fund from Josh Campbell, the father she's never met. The gesture stirs up long-buried questions Harriet had been content to ignore—until now. The time for secrets is over. Harriet is ready to uncover the truth—no matter what she finds.

To Live with a Stranger

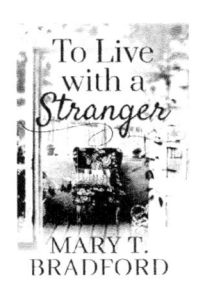

When Cathy Reed and Mark Daniels each inherit Cregane Court, a quaint yet dilapidated cottage in the picturesque village of Ballybawn, they find themselves thrown together by an unusual twist of fate. The inheritance comes with a catch—a challenge laid out in the will. But the biggest hurdle isn't the cottage's state of disrepair; it's Roman O'Driscoll, the estate's solicitor, whose cryptic motives seem bent on discouraging them from accepting their inheritance.

Acknowledgements

This collection holds a special place in my heart for it represents a time in my life that I met a group of people who made my first experience of University a wonderful occasion. I am always thankful to you the readers who continue to support my writing by leaving reviews and telling others about my books. The following I send my thanks and hugs for being so encouraging of this project. My editor and dear friend, Christine who is always there cheering me on. To the amazing authors, Patricia O'Reily, Billy O'Callaghan and Donal Ryan whom I admire so much. Finally to Orla, a lady with much wisdom and patience, and answers every question no matter what I ask, thank you.

Printed in Great Britain
by Amazon